BANK-ROBBERS
AND THE
DETECTIVES.

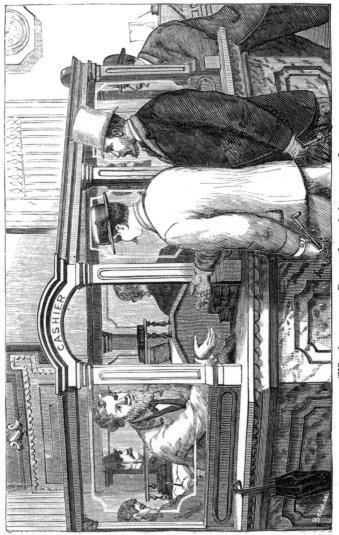

"Why, how are you Barnes, I am glad to see you."

BANK-ROBBERS

AND

THE DETECTIVES.

BY
ALLAN PINKERTON

Black Squirrel Books® 🐿®
an imprint of The Kent State University Press
Kent, Ohio 44242   www.KentStateUniversityPress.com

This facsimile and edition was produced using a scan of a first-edition copy of *Bank-Robbers and the Detectives*. The original edition is part of the Borowitz Collection in the Kent State University Special Collections and Archives and is reproduced with permission.

BLACK SQUIRREL BOOKS® 🐿®
Frisky, industrious black squirrels are a familiar sight on the Kent State University campus and the inspiration for Black Squirrel Books®, a trade imprint of **The Kent State University Press.**
www.KentStateUniversityPress.com

Published by The Kent State University Press, Kent, Ohio 44242
All rights reserved
ISBN 978-1-60635-414-8
Manufactured in the United States of America

First published by G. W. Carleton & Co., Publishers, New York, 1882.

Cataloging information for this title is available at the Library of Congress.

24 23 22 21 20   5 4 3 2 1

EXPLORING THE
BOROWITZ COLLECTION

Cara Gilgenbach
Special Collections and Archives, Kent State University

The Borowitz Collection, from which the editions of the Pinkerton detective stories are taken, was officially gifted to Kent State University in 1989 by Albert and Helen Borowitz of Cleveland, Ohio. The collection includes primary and secondary sources on crime as well as works of literature based on true crime incidents.

Albert and Helen Borowitz, both scholars themselves, built a scholarly collection—one that affords more than sufficient breadth and depth to support any number of research inquiries. The Borowitz Collection reflects the multidisciplinary expertise of Albert Borowitz (a Harvard graduate with degrees in classics, Chinese regional studies, and law) and his late wife, Helen Osterman Borowitz (a Radcliffe graduate and art historian with literary interests). In addition to collecting, Albert Borowitz is himself a scholar of true crime, having published over a dozen books and many articles on the topic, most notably his masterwork, *Blood and Ink: An International Guide to Fact-Based Crime Literature.*

The Borowitz collection is an extensive one, documenting the history of crime, with primary emphasis on the United States, England, France, and Germany from ancient times to the present day. It includes groups of materials on specific criminal cases that have had notable impacts on art, literature, and social attitudes. This provides the researcher with a wealth of material on those cases and their cultural effects. The collection includes nearly 15,000 volumes of books and periodicals, complemented by archival and manuscript collections. Special areas of note include an excellent collection of Sherlock Holmes and other Arthur Conan Doyle early editions; nonfiction and fiction works related to Jack the Ripper; nineteenth- and twentieth-century British and American crime pamphlets and broadsides; a Wild West collection; crime-related photographs, playbills, postcards, and other ephemera; and artifacts, graphics, and memorabilia related to crime.

The Borowitz Collection includes numerous works of detective stories, both fiction and nonfiction, including books from the Pinkerton Detective Agency series, which embody the collection's central theme, namely how real-life elements of crime infiltrate creative works and works of the imagination. Although true crime is the primary focus of the Borowitz Collection, it also contains notable holdings in several other topics and genres, including a vast collection of sheet music spanning more than two centuries of popular musical taste and distinguished literary collections.

The collection provides rich sources to users as diverse as crime historians, film documentarians, museum curators, television and radio producers, antiquarian book dealers, novelists, and faculty and students of history, American studies, women's studies, and criminal justice, to name just a few. Kent State University is proud to steward this collection, and the present project to republish the Pinkerton detective stories is a further outgrowth of our desire to make these interesting and informative resources available to a wider audience.

CONTENTS.

PREFACE.

IN presenting the story of " THE BANK ROBBERS AND THE DETECTIVES," I have attempted to depict an operation which occupied my attention for a long space of time.

From the inception of this case until its conclusion, I never doubted the correctness of my suspicions, or despaired of eventual success, and the result fully proved the fact that on my first examination into the affair I had selected the proper persons upon whom to operate.

The proneness of humanity to temptation is fully exemplified in this case, and while it may occasion some surprise that a man of high social standing, of good business capacity, and enjoying the confidence of the community, should be guilty of the crime for which he was afterwards punished, it is only one more of the many instances which have come under my observation, where an ambition to become suddenly rich and a desire to gratify extravagant tastes have led men, hitherto honorable and upright, to the commission of crimes which have brought shame and disgrace to themselves, and have left the stain of dishonor upon their wives and children.

During the progress of this investigation, I was many times disheartened at the unfortunate operations of circumstances over which I could exercise no control; but in spite of every obstacle I was ultimately successful in maintaining the dignity of law, of capturing the thief, and of restoring to the proper persons nearly the full amount of the money which had been stolen from them.

That this result was accomplished by well-directed and untiring energy, and by a determination not to yield until success was assured, will appear upon a perusal of the narrative, and in the end the convicted man, despondent and despairing, was condemned to long years of imprisonment, and his prospects for life shattered by his own hand.

In all of the incidents related the fictitious has been avoided, and the real and actual only has been recorded.

ALLAN PINKERTON.

CHICAGO, ILLINOIS,
November, 1882.

BANK-ROBBERS

AND

THE DETECTIVES.

———•———

CHAPTER I.

A Mysterious Bank Robbery and an Investigation.

THE business of investigating crime and evil-doing generally, is by no means always active. It has its quiet periods, as have other occupations; but, different from most of these, its seasons of dullness and activity succeed each other with no apparent regularity. Just as merchants at times find themselves pressed with orders beyond their means of supply, and at others are fated to days and weeks of idleness, so with my business; save that mischief throughout the range of my operations seems to be continuous, and even when the people are best behaved, I still find some work to be done.

Early in the spring of 186—, during one of such periods of comparative inactivity, a dispatch was received at the office of my Chicago Agency, requesting my presence at Somerset, Michigan. The brief telegram was as follows:

"First National Bank robbed. Please come, or send, at once.

"THOMAS LOCKE, President."

Happening to be well acquainted with the bank officers through having previously transacted some business for them, and there being nothing special at that time to detain me at headquarters, I started for Somerset the same afternoon: but, owing to detentions, did not arrive at my destination until the next morning.

The weather was clear and the sky balmy when I left Chicago, and I fancied that winter had bid us its annual good-bye. During the single night there had been a wonderfully severe change, however. The clear sky of yesterday had become dull and heavy, its invigorating air had given place to a rude, blustering wind, and a most ugly storm of snow was prevailing.

Four miles of staging from the nearest railroad station, through this raging storm, brought me to the door of the Greyhill House at Somerset. The welcome warmth of a huge stove which furnished the main office of the hotel soon converted the forbidding weather without to a source of enjoyment, by increasing the comforts of shelter, and, as I registered my name and received a kindly greeting from the landlord, I felt that I had stumbled upon a cheery and hospitable inn.

Mr. Locke, and a Mr. Shortridge, respectively the president and the most influential director of the bank, waited upon me at the hotel shortly after my arrival, and at once conducted me to the office of Messrs. Somers and Morton, the bank's counsel.

Mr. Somers, whose more intimate acquaintance the reader will make in the course of this narrative, was a short, thin man, apparently forty years of age. He had a high forehead, deep-set, black lustrous eyes, an aquiline nose and a noticeably large mouth—features usually indicative of a man of pronounced character. Sunken cheeks and a pale complexion told of a consumptive tendency, and a short, hacking cough gave the same testimony. A striking feature in Mr. Somers' personal appearance were the eyebrows. These were black and heavy, and extended across the forehead, so nearly joining in the middle as, at a little distance, to present the illusion of an unbroken arc.

Careful in dress, deliberate in speech, courteous in manner and at all times attentive and observant, Mr. Somers seemed the very type of the successful lawyer.   Entering without preface upon the business in hand, he narrated to me in a clear, methodical way the occurrences which had induced them, as attorneys for the bank, to seek my services.

These were, briefly, that the First National Bank of Somerset had been in some mysterious. way robbed of sixty-five thousand six hundred and twenty-three dollars, and some cents, consisting in large part of United States bonds and notes in a negotiable form, and about five thousand dollars in national bank bills and legal tenders.   Mr. Norton, the cashier, had been detained by some trifling errors in his accounts on Saturday—it was on the following Tuesday that Mr. Somers gave me these facts—until half past ten o'clock at night; an unusually late hour.

The bank occupied as its office a portion of the store of Mr. Henry Sloane—a merchant well established in the hardware business in that town.   On leaving the store, Mr. Norton had seen that everything was secure; a circumstance of which that gentleman, who dropped in before the close of the interview, spoke with great positiveness, supporting the clearness and reliability of his memory by

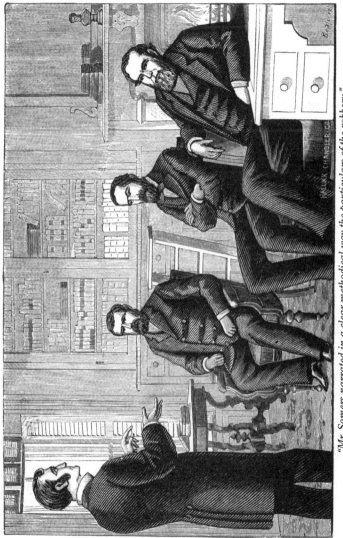

"Mr. Somers narrated in a clear methodical way the particulars of the robbery."

stating how very rare it was for him to be the last to leave the premises.

On opening the safe Monday morning, Mr. Norton discovered to his consternation that the compartment in which was kept all the bank's available reserve had been rifled of its contents. Recovering from the shock which this revelation gave him, he hastened to inform the president and Mr. Somers, who was a director as well as the bank's counsel, of the state of affairs. A consultation between a few of the largest stockholders was held as speedily as possible, with the conclusion that I should be telegraphed for.

When Mr. Somers had finished his narrative, I inquired if any examination of the premises had been made, and upon receiving his reply: "Yes, but without significant result," I told him my first step would be to make such an examination, after which I should wish to interview all who were engaged in the store and bank at the time of the robbery, whether as principals, officers or clerks.

"If you are ready, Mr. Pinkerton, we will step over to the store;" said Mr. Somers. "We feel like pushing this matter; and I presume the less delay the better."

"Exactly," I replied. "Prompt action is often everything in the cases. We will go at once."

The bank was only a few minutes' walk from

the lawyer's offices, but the storm had greatly increased during our consultation, and as we were obliged to face it, the expedition was far from an agreeable one. Mr. Norton, whose feelings seemed wrought up to the highest pitch, seized this opportunity to say :

"I hope, Mr. Pinkerton, you will find it convenient to give this robbery your personal attention. I have heard much of you ; all tending to convince me that if it be possible to unravel the mystery of a crime, you are the man to do it. For my own part I want this pursued relentlessly to the end, cost what it may ; for, until the secret of the robbery is exposed, my position must remain embarrassing and painful. Whatever friends may be good enough to say about it, none will wholly lose sight of the fact that I was last in the store, and that I alone, as a matter of right, know the combination of the safe, without which the safe could not have been entered, except, of course, by force. Mr. Somers is a warm friend of mine, and appreciates fully my feelings in regard to the matter. You may therefore be sure of our heartiest aid in any measures you shall see fit to adopt while pursuing your investigations."

I bowed assent, and Mr. Norton continued :

"I must have my skirts cleared of all suspicion. As matters now are, it is simply horrible. Not only will you suspect me, as it would seem you are bound to do under the circumstances, of which, of course, I have no right to complain, but others, friends whom I shall meet from day to day, will shake their heads when I am away and say : 'I don't know ! It's very queer about that robbery. It's hardly possible that Norton had a hand in it ; but it certainly looks that way. Stranger things *have* happened ; and whoever got the money knew the combination; that's sure !'

"If my wife were to hear talk of that kind, and I am enough of a man of the world to know that there will be plenty of it, I firmly believe it would set her crazy ! But here we are at the store. I hope, with all my heart, you will find some clew."

Mr. Norton's hopes were not realized. A thorough examination of the safe, the office, the store, and the yard at the rear, revealed to me no scrap of evidence that would serve as a clew to the robber or robbers.

The safe lock was in working order and uninjured, save that a small steel plate which covered and protected the back of the lock had been removed and carefully placed in a little unused compartment within the safe. The store doors and their locks were also uninjured. The only inference I could draw from these facts was, that the robbery was *not* the work of professional burglars, but had been committed by some person or persons to whom the combination of the safe had become known.

On our way back to the hotel I asked Mr. Norton if he had any objection to giving me some account of the manner in which he had passed the interval between Saturday night and Sunday morning.

"Not the slightest, Mr. Pinkerton," he answered, with alacrity; "on the contrary, when I have done so I shall be glad to have you ask me every question with regard to myself that may occur to you. I want you to have all the light possible."

Mr. Norton then proceeded to tell me, with much minuteness of detail, that he had gone from the bank on Saturday night directly to his home; had remained within doors with his family until about ten o'clock Sunday morning; had then driven over to Montrose, a town ten miles distant, where his eldest daughter was visiting; had returned with her in the afternoon, and, upon reaching the house, had not again left it until Monday morning, when he went straight to the bank and almost immediately made discovery of the robbery.

During the course of this statement we had reached the Greyhill House and seated ourselves comfortably by a roaring fire in my own apartment. Drawing some cigars from his pocket, Mr. Norton presented me with one, lighted one for himself, and we then continued to talk upon the one theme of interest.

Many suggestions and theories as to who could have committed the robbery were broached by my companion, only to be abandoned as altogether improbable. In shifting about for a subject of suspicion the possibility of an out and out burglary was discussed, and in this connection he told me that Mr. Greene—nominally Mr. Henry Sloane's managing clerk, but in reality his full copartner, sharing with him the profits of the business—claimed to have found some small fibers of wood on the knob of the safe-lock on Monday morning, shortly after the bank's loss became known.

On taking his leave, Mr. Norton again urged me to prosecute my inquiries vigorously, dwelling upon the mortification he must suffer for an indefinite length of time, and giving unmistakable evidence of his anxiety to have the mystery cleared up.

From this interview I learned that all the persons occupied in the hardware store where the

office of the bank was located, were Mr. Henry
Sloane, the proprietor, Mr. George Greene, already named, Mr. B. F. Sloane, familiarly called
"Frank," younger brother to Henry, and the
only regular employee in the establishment, Mr.
Robert Tuttle, paying teller of the bank, and
my informant, Mr. Norton. Mr. Locke, the president, passed much of his time at the bank, but
did not make it his office. Mr. Tuttle was away
on leave of absence on account of ill-health. He
had left a fortnight before and was not expected
back for weeks to come.

Furnished with the foregoing information I received the brothers Sloane and Mr. Greene during
the evening in my rooms at the Greyhill House,
and listened to their several accounts of what
transpired within their knowledge during that
eventful interval.

Of course I used the good opportunities thus
afforded to thoroughly study the faces and bearing of my guests, and perhaps this is as good a
place as I shall find to acquaint the reader with
the results.

Henry Sloane was a quiet, mild-mannered
man, plain in dress and wanting in peculiarities of
appearance on which to found a description. A
well-shaped head, dark hair and beard, the latter
worn full and carefully trimmed, regular features,

a clear complexion of olive tint, and dark hazel eyes, perhaps a little lacking in luster, made up a whole that women would call handsome, and men, good-looking. He told his story in low, measured tones, with so little inflection as to suggest a singular indifference to the whole subject. I afterwards learned, however, that this was his habit.

He had left the store, he said, in company with his brother Frank on Saturday evening; had gone directly home to the house of Mrs. Murdock, where he and Frank boarded, and had remained up until a late hour with Miss Murdock, who that evening accepted his proffer of marriage. This fact Mr. Sloane touched upon without change of manner or voice, as if it were an incidental circumstance not differing in character from any others he mentioned. On Sunday morning, at an exceptionally early hour, he went to the store to give milk to a pet cat, as he was in the habit of doing. He went early because he had a long drive before him immediately after breakfast. To his surprise he found the side door opening upon Willow street ajar. At first he thought robbers might have broken in, but finding the lock all right, and everything about the place undisturbed, he concluded that the open door was due to neglect, and so thought no more about it.

A few days before he had received an urgent letter from his sister Fanny, who was married and lived with her husband at Cloverton, a town some twenty miles distant, inviting him to come over and see them. On leaving the store he went to the house, hurried through breakfast, and then drove to Cloverton. He did not return from that village until Monday noon, when the news of the bank robbery had become noised about everywhere.

Frank Sloane was a tall, well-proportioned young man, of easy address and prepossessing appearance. A slight paleness, possibly on account of some recent illness, possibly an indication of dissipated habits, overspread his face, and a noticeable heaviness of the eyes, gave greater force to the latter surmise. His upper lip was but partly concealed by a light mustache that parted wide in the middle, and waved not ungracefully at the ends. His hair was a thick, glossy brown, and he had a constant habit of running his fingers carelessly through it. He did not appear to be over twenty-two or twenty-three years of age, but was, in reality, as he informed me, in his twenty-ninth year.

For the first few moments in making his statement he displayed considerable embarrassment, and this he endeavored to offset by an affectation of bluntness not natural to him. But after a time his awkwardness wore away, and he became quite at ease, answering the questions I put to him with readiness and apparent candor. He had slept at home Saturday and Sunday nights; on Saturday night with his brother Harry, and on Sunday night alone. He had dropped in at the store on Sunday morning according to habit, and had found the Willow street door open, but surmising that his brother had already been there and had neglected to close it after him, he paid no attention to the circumstance. The rest of the day he had passed about town in saloons and one place and another with several friends, all of whom he named.

In explanation of his visit to the store on Sunday he stated that it was commonly used as a rendezvous on that day by himself and friends.

"Mr. Norton tells me he left the lamp used by him on Saturday at the extreme right hand corner of the desk—is that where you found it?" I asked.

"I don't remember whether I noticed it Saturday night—I mean Sunday morning; but it was there on Monday when I entered the store."

This was an awkward stumble and attracted my attention, notwithstanding my willingness to make large allowance for confusion, natural to most people knowing themselves open to suspicion. In casual conversation such mistakes are of frequent occurrence, and are passed by, as they should be, unheeded. Still, I was not disposed to regard this slip as a mere error of speech. It touched too closely upon the truth I wished to unearth to be lightly regarded; and I therefore made a clear and distinct mental note of the fact.

Mr. Greene was a man of medium height, angular build and wiry frame. He had scarcely arrived at that period of life called "middle-aged," but his hair, considerably tinged with gray, made look much older. His features were sharp and his look penetrating; but the general expression of his face was genial. A high, prominent forehead indicated a fair degree of intelligence which his conversation sustained. One could tell at a glance that he was keen and shrewd, but it was hard to determine whether he was a good-natured, or cold and calculating man.

From the opening of our interview to its close, he was thoroughly self-possessed, answering all my questions in a quick, nervous manner, and looking me straight in the eyes as he did so. He seemed to accept in a business like way the fact that suspicion would rest upon himself in common with all others engaged in the office, or store, and by surmises and suggestions showed great willingness to aid me in my investigations.

The account he gave of his time from Saturday night until Monday morning was explicit and satisfactory. He failed to tell me, however, although otherwise very circumstantial in his narration, the statement he had made to Mr. Norton with regard to the fibers of wood which he claimed to have found upon the knob of the safe-lock.

As I retired for the night I felt that I had heard quite enough of the robbery for one day, and was not sorry that the howling of the wind without, and the pattering of the sleet and hail against my windows, served to distract my thoughts for a time at least from business matters. Presently my fancy groped its way into idle speculations as to the duration of the storm, the hardship it was visiting upon any unprotected wanderer, the possibility that even then it was shielding some midnight plunderers in the perpetration of a dark crime, and so on to crime generally, and to this bank robbery in particular, and then to drowsy wanderings after a clue, in which Greene, fibers of wood, open doors, Frank Sloane, Saturday night and Sunday morning, flitted through my mental vision, and then—sleep.

2

CHAPTER II.

The Investigation Continued.

IN the morning I saw Mr. Somers at the office, and together we went over the whole affair. The theory of a burglary by professional thieves, which had been adopted by some of the bank officers, and had received considerable support from "open door" and "fibers of wood" incidents, was dismissed by me as unworthy of serious consideration. The one important fact with which we had to deal was that the safe had been opened by means of the proper combination.

Believing this to be an inevitable conclusion from all the facts, I asked Mr. Somers if he would be good enough to sketch for me in a general way the character and habits of the three men upon whom suspicion must rest for the present—namely, George Greene and Henry and Frank Sloane ; for Mr. Norton, by reason of unimpeachable integrity, was not to be suspected.

The lawyer's eyes twinkled with satisfaction upon the proffer of my request, and a smile lighted up his face as he gave a ready assent. He had evidently anticipated such a demand, and had prepared himself accordingly ; for he cleared his throat and began in a formal, cut-and-dried style :

"Henry Sloane is a hardware merchant in good standing. Socially he is much respected. He served during the war as a commissioned officer, and is understood to have acquitted himself with credit. About two years since his father died, leaving him some four thousand dollars. A year later he invested a good portion of this money in the business which, in conjunction with George Greene, he still carries on. He has for some time past been paying marked attentions to a Miss Murdock here; and within a day or two I have learned that they are engaged, and that they will be married shortly. Major Murdock, the father of this girl, was killed at the battle of Shiloh. Henry and Frank Sloane were both in the army at the time, and in the same brigade with the major. On their return, after their three years' service, Mrs. Murdock invited them to come and live with her, more for association's sake than anything else, I presume; for her husband left her in very comfortable circumstances. The invitation was accepted, and the boys have still lived there.

"Frank Sloane is known as a 'sporting man.' He volunteered as a private at the outbreak of the war, but soon rose from the ranks and achieved special distinction, being twice promoted for bravery. His good record in the army served to efface, or at least to make amends for, the very bad one he had previously gained. Ten years ago he was arrested for complicity·in a burglary, but through his father's means and influence he was enabled to escape a public trial. The old gentleman never forgave Frank for the disgrace this affair brought upon the family. When on his death-bed, he called me in and divided what property he had, about eight thousand dollars in value, between his elder son, Henry, and his only daughter, Frances, a married lady still residing with her husband at Cloverton.

"The true extent of Frank's criminality, if he was a criminal, was never known ; but the general opinion of the community was that the affair was merely a boyish escapade.

"But since the close of the war Frank has chosen questionable associates, and shown strong tendencies toward a sporting life. He owns a fast horse, which he is almost always willing to back with money ; he attends races whenever opportunity offers ; plays billiards constantly, and drinks freely. His associations are not, however, altogether bad. He goes into good society here, and is well received. The stigma attaching to his ways previous to the war is now pretty well forgotten, or recalled by but few, while his appearance and address make him quite a favorite with most of the young people of our town.

"George Greene is a machinist by trade; is a man of family; is respectably connected, and has lived here about fifteen years. He has had considerable hard luck, and is supposed to be so badly in debt that he finds it best to remain Sloane's silent partner. He has a good character, though, and his troubles seem chiefly to have resulted from heedlessness in money matters—the result of a careless and speculative nature. He stands high in the Masonic fraternity, is a Past Grand Master, or something of that kind, I believe, and is, I know, very popular with that brotherhood."

The forenoon had gone while the lawyer was still talking, and the dinner hour was upon us— a circumstance of which appetite had given due notice. We therefore adjourned our conference and repaired to the Greyhill House, Mr. Somers consenting to be my guest at dinner.

Mr. Somers and the proprietor of the Greyhill, Mr. C. O. Locke, son of Mr. Locke, the bank president, were great friends—a fact that may have insured us more than ordinary hospitality; but, possibly it was owing to his indirect interest in my errand at Somerset that our landlord issued special instructions to the cook in our favor. At all events he gave them, and the result was an excellent dinner; good in the cooking, good in variety, and splendidly served.

While we were smoking our after-dinner cigars the bank directors were holding a meeting in the hotel parlor. Presently we were informed that they had passed a resolution expressive of their unbounded confidence in the integrity of the cashier, Mr. Norton, and had also resolved to refer the whole matter of the robbery to Mr. Somers, with full power to employ such agencies as he might see fit in order to recover the funds of the bank, and bring the thief, or thieves, to justice.

Upon the breaking up of the meeting I met president Locke, Mr. Shortridge, and one or two other of the directors.

"I am very glad, gentlemen," I said, "that you have determined upon so excellent a course. The greatest possible secrecy is one of the first requisites to a successful detective operation. Manifestly, the fewer parties a detective has to deal with in conducting an investigation, the less danger there is that his secrets will become known. Should you require my further services in this case, it will be of very great advantage to me to communicate with Mr. Somers alone; and, I may add, it is desirable that he alone be informed, from time to time, of what progress is being made."

"We shall place our full reliance," said Mr. Shortridge, "on Mr. Somers' judgment in this matter, quite satisfied that it must be far better than that of any of the rest of us, and, since you consider it important, I think we may promise to repress our curiosity as to what is going on until either yourself or Mr. Somers may see fit to inform us. What do you say, gentlemen?" he added, turning to those about him, "isn't that true?"

A general assent was returned; Mr. Norton, who had meanwhile joined us, expressing his concurrence with special heartiness, and the company then separated.

When we were again by ourselves, Mr. Somers bluntly stated that his suspicions rested on Frank Sloane. In support of this opinion he reviewed that young man's career more searchingly than before, and dwelt upon the character of his associates from boyhood as tending to create a generally bad character.

"And in the army," said he, "what reason have we to suppose he was surrounded by better influences? He was adventurous, and justly won promotion by his activity and daring; but this might be as characteristic of a bad man as a good one ; and I have yet to learn that the army was a reformatory school."

"From the manner in which that affair was hushed up," he continued, "it is probable that Frank was actually guilty of the crime with which he was charged when a boy ; and at present he is cheek-by-jowl with Mat. Ray, a known gambler and horse-thief. He is also 'hail fellow well met' with all the bar-room loafers and horse-racing sports of the town. Besides this, he spends a great deal more money than he can honestly earn ; and I need not suggest to you what are the probabilities as to a man's spending his own money for any length of time when persistently associating with people that live by their wits!"

" With regard to Frank Sloane," I replied, "I quite agree with you that he should be held under suspicion until a better subject is presented, or we become satisfied of his innocence. I have noted, however, one or two circumstances in connection with Mr. Greene which call for explanation. The most significant of these is, his omission to say anything to me about finding fibers of wood on the knob of the safe-lock, although he mentioned such an incident to Mr. Norton. It would have been injudicious on my part to call his attention to this discrepancy. If guilty, he would have become suspicious at once, and it is of the greatest importance that whoever the thief may be he should fancy himself unsuspected. The incident itself was of a character not to be readily forgotten. Now, he gave evidence of having a very good memory and I am disposed to set this particular forgetfulness down against him. Furthermore, in my interview with him, I asked if it were possible for any one to learn how to open the safe by watching Mr. Norton when unlocking it. He answered me that he thought not. His opportunities, he said, were better than any one's else, for he was frequently quite close to Mr. Norton at such times waiting for him to get out money for change, or some such matter, and yet he was confident had he tried to discover the combination he would have been unable to do so.

"Now, as a matter of fact, I find that he is mistaken. When the safe was opened in my presence I purposely stood some feet from it, and yet I was able to learn the figures in use, and their order of arrangement. It is true, I could not determine the number of revolutions of the disk prior to each reversal of movement, but these I might soon have learned by experimenting, aided by this knowledge gained through previous observation.

"Thus, Mr. Somers," I continued, "I am unwilling to relieve Mr. Greene from the suspicion which this omission naturally fixes upon him. But, with this reservation, I heartily concur in your view that Frank Sloane is the one on whom suspicion should fall, and the first to be made the subject of close surveillance."

Mr. Somers then informed me that he was resolved to prosecute the matter to the end, regardless of cost. The loss suffered by stockholders was a very severe one, and naturally it was their main object to recover the stolen money; but if there were no hope of getting back a dollar of this, it was still worth while, and was their firm intention, to go to every warrantable expense in order to clear the reputation of all innocent parties, suspected solely on account of their opportunities.

"I make over to you, Mr. Pinkerton," he said in conclusion, "the *carte blanche* I have received from the board of directors, and I will add to it, that I myself will not seek to know anything concerning your plans and operations besides what you choose to tell me."

"Well, you certainly make my task easy at the beginning, Mr. Somers," I answered, "and I am bound to believe that with such an open field before me, and such full authority, I shall not fail of success. I am free to say, however, that the result of my investigation thus far has been anything but satisfactory. I have really nothing on which to build a plausible theory. For some time to come, I fear, we shall have to grope in the dark, and to almost entirely feel our way. In about two weeks I shall send a detective here who will gather and report information that may enable me to fix upon a definite plan of operation. His first duty will be to gain an acquaintance with Frank Sloane, become friendly with him, and win his confidence as far as possible.

"As a preliminary step I would advise that it be given out among the directors, and so allowed to spread itself through the town, that I have been unable to hold out to you any hope of success, and that therefore further investigation of the affair has been abandoned."

Mr. Somers promised that he would carry out this suggestion and promptly advise me if anything new transpired. I then left him, and soon after took my departure for Chicago.

------◆------

CHAPTER III.

A Stranger appears, who Desires to Establish himself in most anything in a Mercantile Way.

TEN days after the events narrated in the previous chapter a young man arrived at Oakdale, a small town on the Great Northern Railroad, about four miles from Somerset, and proceeded to the Robinson House, where he registered as "James Patterson, New York."

He was of medium stature, rather light frame, prepossessing in appearance, and favored with that peculiar, winning expression of the eyes and mouth which enables its possessor to easily gain and retain the esteem of acquaintances. His dress was that of a commercial traveler of the higher grade—quiet, plain and neat, and without peculiarities likely to attract attention.

After dinner Mr. Patterson seated himself near the stove in the main office and gave himself up to the enjoyment of his cigar. The landlord, who was a stout, jolly, sociable fellow, as landlords are in books, and should be in fact, seized the occasion to say a pleasant word to his stranger guest; a civility which was at once rewarded by the offer of a good cigar, which he accepted.

"Business good?" inquired Mr. Patterson.

"Oh, fair, sir, fair," replied the host. "Can't complain, and wouldn't if I could. Are you stopping here for any length of time, sir?"

"Well, I really don't know. I left New York some weeks ago and have been halting at different towns on the route with some notion of locating, if I can find the right place."

"You oughtn't to leave our town without

giving it a fair trial. What line of business, may I ask ?''

"Oh, most anything in a mercantile way," answered Mr. Patterson. "I have been a commercial traveler for years, and I've got an idea that with my general knowledge of business and a little capital, I shall be ready to take hold of the first good thing that offers."

"Exactly," rejoined the landlord. "If you conclude to put up here for a while, I shall be glad to show you about town and introduce you to some of our people."

"Thank you. I've pretty much made up my mind to remain here for a week or two at all events. I like the looks of the place, and would remain permanently if I could find a favorable opening."

The landlord, who was named Smith, and his guest then engaged in more detailed talk regarding business prospects, during which they became pretty well acquainted. Mr. Patterson found that Mr. Smith possessed about all the information he desired. Mr. Smith found Mr. Patterson a most agreeable and entertaining gentleman ; and when their conversation was brought to a close, each expressed his gratification that they had met.

Just before dusk the Somerset stage came

rattling along the road and was driven up to the Robinson House piazza, where Mr. Patterson happened to be standing.

"Been warming up your horses a trifle, driver?" queried Mr. Patterson, in a familiar way.

"Faith, sir, its thimsel's has done the warmin'," responded the driver, who was everywhere known as "good-natured Sam;" "that tame don't need no dhriver, sir. A brakeman's all *they* want!"

"They certainly look like good stock," rejoined Mr. Patterson; "and how about the driver? Is he warmed up, too?"

"It *is* a purty cold day an' no mistake;" returned Sam, with true Irish shrewdness.

"Then let's go inside and have a good hot whiskey," said Mr. Patterson with an amused smile. "That would balance accounts with the weather, wouldn't it?"

In the bar-room of the hotel two smoking hot drinks were soon placed before these new acquaintances, who had seated themselves at a small table that they might, as Patterson expressed it, "take their toddies in comfort." Over these the pair grew communicative and friendly. Sam soon found to his delight that the stranger was an appreciative listener, and he took advantage of the discovery to pour into his ear many an anecdote

of the residents of Oakdale and Somerset. Mr.
Patterson had little occasion to say anything, but
always saw that Sam's glass was refilled whenever
there seemed a possibility of a pause in his remarks.

On parting from his sociable friend, probably
as a return compliment, Sam warmly invited him
to accompany him to Somerset in the morning,
offering him the inducement that it would cost him
nothing there and back.

"No, thank you, Sam," said Mr. Patterson ;
"not to-morrow. Some day I may take a run over
there with you, for you have quite interested me
in the place.   But just now I am looking about for
business here ; and 'Im one of those who believe
in business before pleasure."

"Faith it's a good rule, sir !   Thin I'll be ready
for you ony time, Mr. Pattherson, 'n' plazed to hev
the honor of your company."   So saying, Sam
bowed politely and took his departure.

During the evening Mr. Smith and Mr. Patterson chatted together for some time, and improved
the acquaintance so satisfactorily begun earlier in
the day.   The landlord wished that his guest had
arrived two days earlier that he might have attended a ball given at the Robinson House.

"It was a grand success, and we had all the

best people of the two towns with us," he remarked, with a touch of excusable pride.

"Well, I am sorry I missed so much," rejoined
Mr. Patterson. "I know I should have enjoyed
it. Is the season for these parties over now ?"

"Oh, no," replied the landlord ; "by no means,
sir. We shall have plenty more of 'em. There'll
be one at Somerset within a few days, and you
must certainly go. I don't know just when it's
going to take place ; but it'll surely pay you to
wait for it."

A day or two after Mr. Patterson's arrival at
Oakdale, he was strolling about the village when
a gentleman accosted him with the remark :

"Surely I have met you before, sir ?"

"Your face certainly seems familiar to me, but
I can't place it. I'm from New York," responded
Patterson.

"I thought so," said the stranger. "My
name's Russell. I'm traveling for Tracy & Co.
Ever hear of 'em."

"Why, I used to travel for them," threw out
Mr. Patterson. "Still, I don't distinctly recall
you. Have you been with Tracy long ?"

"Not quite a year," replied Mr. Russell
"What do you say," he added, "to stepping
across the way—I see a saloon there—to see

if we can't find something to refresh our minds as well as our stomachs?"

"The experiment is worth trying," said Mr. Patterson, lightly, "though, if you will allow me, a better plan would be for you to join me at the Robinson House, where I am staying. It's only a step, and I know the liquors to be first-class there."

"Anything'll suit me that's got good liquor in it," replied the commercial traveler as he took his companion familiarly by the arm, and they together proceeded to the hotel.

Over their drinks Mr. Russell and Mr. Patterson began to feel sure that they were old acquaintances. It was never exactly settled when or where they had met, but the fact gradually came to be accepted as established. In the course of conversation it appeared that Mr. Russell was well acquainted in Somerset, and had several good customers there whom he intended visiting on the next day. He said that Somerset was a much livelier place than Oakdale, though it was off the line of the railroad. If Patterson wished, he would be glad to introduce him to some of the business men there, and he might like the place and people so well that he would find it the very spot he was looking for. Finally he insisted that his friend should take the stage with him the next morning, saying he would not take "no" for an answer.

Mr. Patterson was sorry to resist so pressing an invitation, especially one so attractive in every way, but had made engagements in Oakdale that would so take up his time that he must deny himself the present pleasure of visiting Somerset. He would, however, go over there within a day or two, and hoped Mr. Russell's stay would be long enough to enable them to meet again.

The two traveling salesmen passed a good part of the day together, playing billiards, smoking, and becoming better acquainted in different ways, so that by night they were very intimate.

On the next day Mr. Russell took the stage for Somerset as intended, and the following day good-natured Sam was much pleased to learn that his liberal, gentlemanly friend, Mr. Patterson, was to be one of his passengers. They had sipped many another hot whiskey since their first meeting, and as Sam had once or twice been permitted to do the treating, he conceived a high opinion of Mr. Patterson's manners, and spoke of him as "a gintleman, every inch of him."

When the stage was ready Mr. Patterson took a seat outside with the driver, and had soon bettered himself still further in his good opinion by sundry intelligent remarks regarding the team, which was a splendid one, and concerning Sam's driving, which was equally as good.

On their arrival at the Greyhill House, Mr. Russell at once took possession of his New York friend and insisted on his taking a stroll about town. Every one they met seemed to know Mr. Russell, and when any one stopped to exchange a word, the latter would introduce his companion as "an old friend of mine from New York—used to work for Tracy & Co., too!"

Mr. Patterson had assented to these proceedings with some apparent reluctance, but when Mr. Russell proposed to go to Sloane's hardware store, he objected outright, and excused himself on the ground that he had left Sam, the driver, at the hotel somewhat abruptly, and as he was, so to speak, his guest on this occasion, he owed him better treatment. Leaving his friend with this explanation, the visitor from Oakdale returned to the Greyhill House, and in the afternoon took the stage back to the latter village.

Mr. Patterson, who was of course my detective, had acted thoroughly up to my instructions to make his meeting with the Sloanes purely accidental ; for it would be extremely unwise to seem to seek the parties he was to operate against, even when screened by an introduction from one so peculiarly well fitted to give it as Russell.

On my detective's return to Oakdale, Mr. Smith informed him that the day for the ball at

Somerset had been fixed upon; that Frank Sloane had been there distributing invitations, and had left one especially for Mr. Patterson, as a friend of his, Mr. Smith's.

"The ball is to take place a week from to-morrow," concluded Mr. Smith, "and you must come."

Patterson went over to Somerset again the following day with a Captain Maynard, a resident of Oakdale, to whom Mr. Smith had introduced him. While standing at the bar of the Greyhill House awaiting the preparation of some drinks, Mr. Russell made his appearance accompanied by two friends. As soon as he caught sight of Patterson he rushed forward and shook him cordially by the hand after the manner of an old friend. He then presented his companions as Mr. Greene and Mr. Frank Sloane. Capt. Maynard, who knew Russell slightly, and the other two gentlemen well, changed his instructions to the bar-tender to meet the requirements of the whole party, without waiting to know whether the new-comers would drink or not. It was evident he knew something of the tastes of his friends, for he ordered whiskey straight for them, and no one whispered an objection. The drinks were but just consumed when Mr. Russell insisted upon returning the compliment, after which Patterson took

"He then presented his companions."

his turn and Greene and Sloane followed in quick succession.

A running fire of conversation was kept up over these drinks, chiefly by Russell, Sloane and Patterson, and took the character of light, jesting chatting, with an occasional good joke; a line in which Sloane was quite proficient. Russell was very talkative and took the floor at every opportunity. He had already been imbibing when the party met, and this accounted to Patterson for his rather singular warmth of greeting.

"We expect to have a ball here two weeks from to-night, Mr. Patterson," said Frank Sloane, taking that gentleman aside. "We shall be real glad of your company. Will you come?"

"Thank you," rejoined Patterson, "but I understood him it was to be a week from to-day."

"It's a weakness of Smith's to get things mixed up," said Sloane, "and you see how near he came to it this time. I told him my brother's wedding was two weeks from to-day, and the ball only one week."

"I hardly know whether I shall stay so long in these parts," returned Patterson. "I am looking about in a business way at Oakdale. I haven't found anything there to tempt me to stay, except a first-class hotel and some pleasant people. This is all well enough in its way, but it don't line one's pockets."

"Why don't you come over here to Somerset ? This is just the place for an enterprising man. Oakdale is our railroad station, and that's about all you can say for it. Remain here until the ball, and I'll guarantee something will turn up in the meantime to suit you exactly ; but you ought to put up here at the Greyhill. Smith is a splendid fellow and keeps a good hotel, but this is the spot for a live man with brains and money."

It was evident that the talkative proprietor of the Robinson House had been doing my detective good service all unknown to himself, in his conversation with Frank Sloane.

"I can't say that I can boast of having much of a supply of either," said Patterson, with a smile intended to belie his words. "But I would like to attend this ball, and must manage somehow to do so."

"Well then, that's all settled !" rejoined Sloane, who was sufficiently affected by the liquor to make him persistent. "Now the question is : Oakdale against Somerset. What do you say ?"

"That the proposition strikes me favorably," replied Patterson with an air of hesitation.

"That's not to the point," rejoined Sloane. "Say you'll come, now, and be done with it !"

"Perhaps a little more of that whiskey would help settle it," broke in Patterson, laughingly, approaching the others as he spoke. "What do you say, gentlemen, one more round for a finish?"

"One more, boys, by all means," said Russell.

"And then good-bye by no means," chimed in Sloane. "What's the hurry?"

"It's time for the stage, and I must be going," said Patterson, as he gave the requisite nod to the barkeeper.

"Yes, and I must go down with you," said Russell.

Glasses were once more filled and drained of their contents. Dancing eyes, and voluble talk, with a slight trace of thickness in it, now showed that some, at least, of the party, had had more than was good for them, and warned the more prudent that it was time to discontinue the roystering.

Fifteen minutes later Patterson and Russell were on their way back to Oakdale. On their arrival, Russell, who had concluded his business in that locality, took a westward-bound train, bidding his companion a hearty good-bye, and wishing him every success.

Such was the first meeting between my detective and those whose acquaintance he was instructed to make, with a view of thoroughly ingra-

tiating himself into their confidence.   It could
hardly have been brought about more favorably.
Russell's error as to Patterson's identity may
seem singular at first, but a second thought will
remind the reader that such an opportunity is an
every-day occurrence, and that this one differed
from the commonplace event in result only in
Patterson's taking advantage of the commercial
traveler's mistake, and in artfully handling this
false impression until it became belief, and final
conviction.

The great benefit to the Agency arising from
such an introduction as Patterson had received
must be apparent.

If either Frank Sloane or Greene were concerned in the robbery, or had any guilty knowledge of it, they would naturally be on the look-
out for detectives, and would be suspicious of any
stranger who might come to Somerset.   This suspicion could now hardly arise with reference to
Patterson, unless some unfortunate circumstances
should give it birth, for his introduction to them
took place in a natural way, and through the instrumentality of an old acquaintance, who, probably, knew little, and cared less, about the robbery, and could not be suspected of assisting in
placing a detective on the ground.

I was, of course, in constant communication

with Patterson, furnishing him with such instructions as the situation seemed to call for; and, at
this point, I planned his operations for the immediate future, directing him to give most of his
attention to Mr. Frank Sloane, on whom, after a
full survey of the facts in my possession, I was
willing the burden of suspicion should continue
to fall.

True, Mr. Greene came in for an almost equal
share of distrust, but if he were the guilty party,
he was also the one less likely to squander or lose
the stolen funds, and, therefore, it would be better
to leave his case until satisfied of the other's innocence.

While Patterson was still at Oakdale, I learned
from Mr. Somers that he had carried out his part
of his programme, and that it was now pretty
generally understood that all attempts to discover
the criminals had been abandoned, inasmuch as
the detectives were unable to find any clew. Some
surprise was expressed that the matter should be
given up so tamely, but it was answered that the
loss was a very heavy one, and that the stockholders were unwilling to add to it by enriching
detectives who could not hold out even a hope of
success.

When it is remembered that no director other
than Mr. Somers knew this to be untrue, it will

3

be understood how easily such an impression could be given out, the directors themselves unconsciously acting as agents in circulating the excusable falsehood.

———◆———

CHAPTER IV.

Somerset is Provided with an Enterprising Insurance Agent.

A VILLAGE ball is something that the general reader cannot be greatly interested in ; and the Somerset party, the discussion of, and preparations for which had brought my detective into somewhat closer relations to those whom he most desired to cultivate, would have had no earthly interest for me, had it not served to still further fix Mr. Patterson in the good opinion of the people of that village, and bring to light a few of the characteristics of the persons with whom he would be obliged to keep close company in the future.

It certainly brought together the best people of the place, and Somerset contained a number of wealthy and refined families. It secured for Detective Patterson an unexcelled chance to study them and estimate how much confidence he could place in this one, or how careful he must be to avoid another one's enmity ; how such a family's friendship might aid him in gaining the general respect of the townspeople, and how another family's friendship might compromise his standing.

Besides, as he was fortunate enough to secure a large number of introductions, and, through Sloane's and Greene's mutual interest in him, found himself engaged for nearly every set with some interesting single or married lady, he found it a very simple matter to establish a thorough conviction that he was almost totally ignorant of the details of the bank robbery ; and quite as easy to gather up and classify the different theories held as to the perpetration of the crime, as well as to secure much other valuable information for future use ; so that altogether, the Somerset ball, coming as it did so soon after my operative's arrival in the place, proved a second circumstance as greatly in our favor as Patterson's hearty indorsement by Russell ; for it gave him quite as cordial an entrance into the best society of the village, in a way which could not possibly suggest a suspicion of his being a detective—as this hearty introduction and indorsement had come from the very persons whose supposed guilt he had been detailed to unearth.

The day following the ball, Patterson was standing on the piazza of the Robinson House, conversing with the landlord, when the stage drove up and Frank Sloane and a Mr. Morgan alighted. After some little talk about the enjoyments of the previous evening, Sloane said :

"Jim, I think I've found something that would suit you. Morgan, here, is in the insurance business, and don't more than half like it. Why not make some arrangement with him ?"

"Frank is a little too fast, Mr. Patterson," broke in Mr. Morgan. "I like the business well enough, but I haven't time to properly attend to it. Perhaps we might come to some terms, if you are looking for business, that would pay us both."

"The fact is," replied my detective, "I have been a dry-goods salesman, and my inclination naturally gives me a preference for that line of business ; but if I could see a good prospect in this, I don't know any reason why I should not take hold of it. I shall be glad to talk the matter over with you. When I see your figures I shall be ready with an answer."

The interval of delay thus secured was used by Patterson to advise my Chicago superintendent of the proposition, which he authorized him to at once accept, if favorable terms could be secured. Ten days after the sign of "Patterson & Morgan," insurance agents for several well-known eastern companies, was displayed on Main street, Somerset, and my detective took up his residence at the Greyhill House.

Spring had nearly gone when I had next returned from Chicago from supervising important operations at my eastern agencies. It had not been deemed worth while to advise me as to the Somerset matters during my absence, no developments of special importance having transpired. I, therefore, found a great mass of reports and correspondence on hand for my revision.

From these I learned that Patterson had been steadily progressing in Frank Sloane's confidence. The two played billiards together almost daily; made evening calls together; went out driving, hunting and fishing together; and, to all appearances, were the closest friends.

Patterson's reports abounded with illustrations of his companion's character, and these showed it not to differ from my first estimate of it. He was an out-spoken, open-hearted, devil-may-care fellow, fond of having what is called "a good time," it mattered but little how he got it.

He talked freely about the robbery, but apparently knew no more about it than had come to light in a public way.

"It's a great mystery," he would say, "and I don't believe they'll ever find out who got the money. I know one thing; if I had done the job, no one should ever know it; that's sure!"

Greene had occasionally shown himself more sociable than usual with him; had at times played billiards and drank with my detective; and had twice invited him to his house; yet his manner was so studiously reserved that Patterson was strongly inclined to transfer his suspicions, and had asked the Agency's permission to give more of his time and attention to Greene. A circumstance had occurred just before my return which served to hasten this move, and it had been determined to act accordingly.

About two weeks subsequent to the robbery Mr. Somers had written to the Agency that Greene had that day handed him a small piece of iron which he claimed to have extracted from the lock of the store-door opening on Willow street. Greene said that the lock would not work; that he took it to pieces and found the bit of iron inside, and that he thought it was a portion of a skeleton key. Mr. Somers had forwarded the piece of metal and it had proven to be steel instead of iron.

This incident of itself was trifling; but it

subsequently obtained significance from the way it was communicated to my detective.

The subject of the robbery came up one day in the presence of Greene and Patterson, being introduced by a third party, one Dr. Hammond, when Greene volunteered the statement that he found a piece of skeleton key in the lock of this Willow street door on the Thursday following the mysterious disappearance of the bank's funds—which was the day after my departure from Somerset—and that this circumstance satisfied him that the robbery was committed by professional burglars.

If Greene had really found the piece of metal so soon after the robbery it would seem that he would have at once made the fact known to Mr. Somers. Again, if he had discovered it at the time he spoke to Mr. Somers about it—nearly two weeks later—it is singular that he should have made such an error as to date when recounting the incident in Patterson's presence. Besides, as has been said, the piece of metal was of steel. Now, skeleton keys are not made of steel, but of soft iron, and this fact suggested whether the steel instrument had ever been in the lock at all. I did not believe that it had.

These considerations convinced me that there was something wrong with this, cold, keen and reserved Mr. Greene. There was no reason, however, for relieving Frank Sloane from surveillance; but this should be made only secondary to that which ought to be exercised over Mr. Sloane's "silent partner."

He would undoubtedly prove a hard subject to work upon; for, though displaying no particular aversion to talking about the robbery, he never himself introduced the topic, and on one occasion had shown considerable sensitiveness regarding it.

A friendly party were at the Greyhill saloon and were "chaffing" each other in a harmless way, when one of them said to Greene, in retaliation for some jesting slur by the latter upon his integrity:

"Oh, that's nothing; not half so bad as getting a bank into your store, and then robbing it!"

Greene flushed at the remark, and answered, with more bluntness than was common to him: "Shut up!—won't you?" at the same time flinging a book at the speaker, and laughing away his confusion as best he could.

This confusion *might* have arisen either from the sensitiveness of one who felt that so long as the crime remained a mystery, all who might have committed it were open to suspicion; or, from the agitation of conscious guilt. It would hardly have been worthy of note had there not been other circumstances indicating Greene's guilt.

Shortly after my return I received a letter from Mr. Somers, asking my opinion as to the present aspects of the case, and stating that he would like to have some definite knowledge of the progress already made; that he had every confidence in my ability to do what could be done; and was willing, if I distinctly advised it, to continue the investigation as long as need be; but if no good prospect of ultimate success were yet in view, he was ready to abandon, or, at least discontinue the operation; that the matter of expense was becoming serious; and it was not probable that he could much longer keep the directors in ignorance of what was being done, as they were becoming impatient. He slyly hinted that he felt sure my detective was in Somerset, and in the insurance business; as such a party, named Patterson, had recently established himself there, and had become quite friendly with Frank Sloane. If his surmise was correct, he desired to be put into communication with Mr. Patterson, or at least have that gentleman authoritatively known to him, that he might assist him, if occasion required.

To this letter I replied in reassuring terms, stating that I was well satisfied with the present

3*

status of affairs, and only expected success
through a long and tedious operation. I informed
him of the degree of intimacy existing between
Frank Sloane and my detective, Mr. Patterson,
and of my increasing suspicion that Mr. George
Greene was the real culprit, and Sloane, if connected with the affair at all, but an accessory.

I then advised Patterson that the proposed
change of base was agreed upon, and directed him
to write me fully as to Greene's character so that
I might devise some plan for overreaching him.
A reply soon came to hand, stating that Greene
was a thorough business man, wary, cautious and
reserved. He prided himself on his penetration and
knowledge of the world, one of his favorite expressions being: "You've got to get up early to
waken me !" Much of his time was given to Masonic lodge meetings, making it difficult to secure his
frequent companionship ; and occasionally in his
more genial moods he had proposed to Patterson
that he should become a Mason ; but though my
operative wrote that he was certain this course
would bring him into so intimate relations with
Greene that he could worm his secret from him, I
could not favor so questionable a proceeding. At
the close of his letter was this paragraph, which
I at once seized upon as the key to the situation.

"Greene sometimes talks 'poor.' I think he

would like to borrow. I am supposed to have some idle means. Would it not be well to lead him on to borrowing of me? This could easily be done, and lending him money would surely remove any doubt about my being what I represent."

"To the extent that the firm's responsibility will justify," I answered, "lend Greene, on business account, what he may require. If the bank should be too timid to make the advance, I will do so myself; for I see in this project a remote solution of the mystery."

To the north of Somerset a well-wooded hill rises with some abruptness, and at its foot is a fine stream having its source in a small body of water, a few miles distant, called Duck Lake. Trouting in this stream or hunting in the surrounding woods were favorite sports with the young men of both Somerset and Oakdale. Frank Sloane was much given to these rambles, and latterly Greene and Patterson had accompanied him.

One day, as these three were returning from a rather fruitless expedition, Frank exclaimed:

"By Jove, boys! this is a sorry day's work. Altogether we've hardly enough for a good meal."

"About as good as the hardware business

nowadays, anyhow!" said Greene. "We work all day at that for nothing."

"Why, I thought 'business was always good in Somerset,'" broke in Patterson, quoting an expression that had frequently been used to induce him to locate there.

"So it is—on paper," retorted Greene. "Our books show well enough, but the people all seem to buy with no idea of paying until they get ready."

"I thought the people about here were 'good pay,'" said Patterson. "I hope so, for we have been rather careless in collecting premiums lately."

"You needn't trouble yourself about that," said Greene. "A really bad debt is almost unknown in this region ; but times have been so hard that our customers are constantly asking for extensions. Then Harry and I have been laying in a pretty large stock ; so that for a time our candle has been burning at both ends."

"Look out, Jim ! That kind of talk means : 'Pity the sorrows of a poor old man !' as sure as my name's Frank Sloane," exclaimed that young gentlemen.

"I shouldn't be very badly scared if it did," replied Patterson. "I know what it is to be hard pushed in money matters myself."

"Frank told about the truth, Patterson," said

Greene, seemingly relieved by my operative's remark. " It never occurred to me to apply to you,
but if you can help us over this period of slow
payments, you shall have good interest, and you
would be doing us a very great favor besides."

" Call and see me at the office to-morrow," said
Patterson. "I have some money on hand, and
perhaps I can accommodate you."

Greene quite naturally became more friendly
in his manner as they pursued their way homeward, and for the first time made frequent use of
Patterson's Christian name. Passing Mrs. Murdock's, where Frank Sloane left them, he accompanied my detective to the Greyhill House, where
he insisted on opening a bottle of wine. Over this
he stated that the amount needed by the firm was
fifteen hundred dollars, for which he would give
Henry Sloane's note, indorsed by himself. Patterson promised that he should have the money the
following day, and they parted with great cordial-
ity, " Jim " and " George " henceforth to the end
of their acquaintance.

As soon as Greene was out of the way Patterson telegraphed the agency for the amount he had
engaged to lend ; arrangements were at once made
by wire with Mr. Somers to place the same at the
former's disposition, and at the designated time
the transaction was completed.

Subsequent reports demonstrated that this loan had effectually secured Greene's friendship. He now dropped in at Patterson's office whenever passing; invited him to his own store repeatedly; often proposed having a social drink; and in every way evinced a genuine desire to become intimate. Greene was as much devoted to billiards as Frank Sloane, and it became quite common for him to call on Patterson at the hotel and engage in that pastime. Occasionally, through my detective's artifices, their conversation would touch upon the subject of the robbery, but when the matter was fairly broached, Greene would become reserved and silent.

Once, however, my detective, tired of the unsuccessful results of his efforts, boldly asked Greene if any attempt had ever been made to discover the criminal. They were seated in the hardware store alone, the Sloane brothers having gone to dinner. Singularly enough, Greene had paved the way to this question by referring to Mr. Tuttle, whose death had just been reported at Somerset.

Patterson pretended to know nothing of Tuttle, and Greene had explained that he was a clerk in the bank, who had left shortly before the robbery on account of ill-health.

"Yes," said Greene, in reply to the question

Patterson had then put, "Mr. Pinkerton came down here and returned without accomplishing anything. He interviewed me for over an hour, and said at the close that my statement made his trouble just so much less, as it took me completely out of the list of those who might be suspected. He was quite confidential with me. He told me that he received five hundred dollars for making the examination, whether anything was discovered or not, but was afraid that would be the end of it, as he had examined every one who might have been concerned, and all made a clear showing."

It is needless to say these statements were pure invention on the part of Greene. It is against my life-long practice to commit myself in any such way. Nor do I ever ask any sort of a fee for beginning an investigation. My terms are invariably so much per day for every man engaged—a given rate for operatives' services, and a given rate for my own or those of my superintendents.

I could not imagine why Greene should have found it worth while to invent these falsehoods. Did he suspect Patterson to be a detective? Had he told him these things, watching the effect produced, in the hope that my detective would betray himself? This could hardly be, for by such experimenting, if his suspicions were well founded,

he would surely convict himself of misrepresenta-
tion. But if he regarded Patterson as an ordinary
business and social acquaintance, one to whom he
was obligated, and for whom he felt some friendship, why should he attempt to deceive him with
such a story? No explanation consistent with
Greene's innocence occurred to me. So far as I
knew he was not a common liar. Patterson's reports had not indicated that he was a man of that
stamp, but rather described him as a shrewd, reserved gentleman. Since their increasing intimacy,
however, my detective had discovered that Greene,
when drinking, and Greene, thoroughly sober,
were two very different persons; the one, all genial
and friendly; the other, cold, distant and formal.
They had been drinking somewhat freely on the
occasion mentioned, and that might have accounted for Greene's misstatements.

After puzzling over the matter for a long time
I found myself forced to this conclusion: either
Greene, as a party to the robbery, had invented
this pretended conversation with me in order to
screen himself; or else, being innocent, he had
wished to stand well in Patterson's regard and had
resorted to fiction in order to compliment himself,
and remove any possible distrust his friend might
entertain.

Abandoning the second opinion as without support, I now became fully satisfied that Greene was the party we wanted, and issued instructions to Patterson to such effect, urging him to redouble his caution while pressing investigation in that direction.

CHAPTER V.

Plotting and Planning.

TOWARD the latter part of May Mr. Somers somewhat unexpectedly called upon me at my office in Chicago, for the purpose, he said, of furnishing me with important information connected with the robbery, which he felt confident would lead to the discovery of the criminals. Without unnecessary preface he told me that a letter had recently fallen into his hands purporting to have been written by a man named Hennessy, who was then serving a long term of imprisonment for burglary in the Michigan penitentiary at Jackson. The letter was addressed to an old comrade of Hennessy's, named Powers, and stated that the writer knew who committed the Somerset robbery, and would tell what he knew, if by so doing he could secure his own pardon. Powers was asked to see the proper persons and, if possible, enter into an arrangement with them.

Having told me so much, Mr. Somers submitted the letter for my inspection with the remark that it had been inclosed in a second envelope and thrust through the letter-drop of his
office. I read the letter carefully, found it to
bear all the marks of a genuine production and
accepted it as such. Mr. Somers could give me
very little information about Powers beyond the
facts that he was a rascally fellow without character, and lived in the country, a few miles from
Somerset.

I then told my client that I had but little faith
in revelations of this kind; that convicts would
ordinarily do, or promise, anything that might
possibly release them. The game was as old as
imprisonment itself, but so rarely resulted satisfactorily, that I could hardly recall an instance in
which such pretended disclosures had proven
true.

Notwithstanding this, Mr. Somers felt satisfied
that there was something in it, and asked if it
would interfere with my plans should he pursue
an inquiry in that direction. I replied that it
would not; that I quite approved of learning
more concerning these two men, Hennessy and
Powers, so far as could be done with absolute secrecy; that it would not do to permit the fact that
investigation was still going on, to leak out; and

that it would be well to accept with many grains of salt whatever these men might say. On the whole I concluded that Patterson could best conduct the affair, and promised to put it in his charge.

I was glad to learn from Mr. Somers that my detective stood well in the community; that he was a welcome visitor at the Talcott's, the Murdock's and the Shortridge's, and so on; that socially he was much respected; and that among business men his bearing and repute were excellent. Mr. Somers had heard some whispers as to his being a detective, but they had quickly, and long before, died out, and it now seemed impossible that such a thought could cross the minds of any.

We then compared notes with regard to the evidence already gathered, and Mr. Somers fully concurred in the opinion that, if Hennessy could throw no light on the matter, the burden of suspicion should rest on Greene. I again informed Mr. Somers that the case would doubtless prove a long one, since Greene avoided the subject of the robbery with persistent and suspicious care; and that it might be necessary to devise some plan for forcing from him any secrets he might possess. I would think this over, I said, and as soon as anything occurred to me, would let him know of it, so that, if advisable, concerted action might be had.

A day or two after Mr. Somers' visit, I learned from Patterson that Frank Sloane contemplated attending some races about to take place at Roslyn, Indiana, and that Matt Ray, a man of bad repute, was to accompany him. Patterson wrote that the invitation had first been extended to him ; but, not feeling at liberty to leave Greene, he had declined it.

On receipt of this information, which was given with full details about route and time, I sent two detectives to intercept Sloane on the way, and thereafter to keep him in sight and report fully his every action.   They were furnished with hand-bills offering ten thousand dollars reward for information leading to the arrest and conviction of the perpetrators of a certain robbery, with instructions to place one of the same where it might fall under the eye of young Sloane.   Date and locality were torn from these placards, the only purpose of their use being to keep fresh in Sloane's mind the Somerset robbery, and excite his cupidity in case he had any secret knowledge of it.   This scheme, however, was unsuccessful.   Under the impulse of a mere whim, Sloane and Ray changed the projected route at the last moment, and so evaded my detectives.

While Frank was away, Henry Sloane suddenly started for Canada, giving out that he was called there by losses in oil wells in which he was interested. I thought it rather strange that he should leave the store while Frank was absent, especially as the latter was to be gone but three days. Henry's departure was too sudden, however, to permit of his being watched ; and I found myself obliged to await his return in order to test the truth of the story about oil wells.

His delay was protracted several days beyond expectation. It appeared on his return that he had been detained at London, Canada, by arrest on a writ of *capias*, for a debt of three hundred dollars ; a lien against an oil well of which he was part owner. Sloane stated that he was compelled to borrow the money in order to secure his release. In casual conversations Patterson picked up much incidental confirmation of this account, of itself reasonable enough, but, not satisfied with anything short of certainty, I wrote to a correspondent at London, who, in due course of mail, verified it fully.

All this time Patterson was prosecuting the insurance business steadily, giving it the fullest attention consistent with his chief purpose. I was gratified to receive accounts from him showing that his profits more than covered his entire expenses in the interest of the operation, for these had been exceptionally large. In order to secure the constant companionship of Greene and Sloane he was obliged to keep pace with them in their pleasure-seeking, and this entailed much liquor drinking, smoking and billiard playing, with frequent attendance at plays and concerts when traveling companies visited the town.

But though all this was expensive, it was absolutely necessary, and was not without its good results in many directions.

Patterson grew to be a genuine favorite in Somerset, and his society was not only welcomed but really sought after by the best people of the place, who had good reason to believe him an accomplished young man, with a sufficient amount of ready money to choose his business, and plenty of interest-bearing investments to make it quite unnecessary for him to work at all.

When, then, they saw how energetically he applied himself to what he had undertaken, making more in a month out of insurance than Mr. Morgan had made in a year, they considered him an exceptionally excellent addition to the business and social circles of the place; so that being compelled by his desire to keep as nearly as possible constantly with Greene and the Sloanes, the society of the young ladies of the place, where he was naturally considered a good "catch," was forced upon him, and, very like any other young man of good parts, he enjoyed himself as much as possible while attending strictly to his business.

As the Sloanes lived, rather than boarded, at Mrs. Murdock's, Henry having married one of her daughters, and the other, a bright, handsome girl, being still unmarried and at home, my detective, in seeking Frank's company, became very intimate with this young lady, and, in all their pleasure excursions claimed and secured her company. This fact on one occasion led to a little revelation that had a rather important bearing upon the operation.

One evening when several couples were on their way to a neighboring town for a quiet pleasure trip, and a drive home in the pleasant moonlight, as usual, Patterson accompanied Miss Nellie Murdock, and it is by no means improbable, as would have been the case with other young couples, that many things were said which may as well remain unsaid here.

This fact, however, came to the surface from little hints thrown out by Miss Murdock, which were gradually shaped into a regular confession by my artful detective.

On Patterson's arrival in Somerset, Greene had hinted that he was a detective "working up the bank case," and, whenever opportunity occurred, rather sneered at his business pretensions. The Sloanes and Murdocks doubting this, and being very favorably impressed with my detective, were quite indignant at the charge. Miss Murdock further stated, with much satisfaction, that Greene had then written to Mr. Russell, Tracy & Co.'s commercial traveler, who had introduced Patterson at Somerset, and had received a reply that entirely upset his theories and suspicions, when he had been fair enough to acknowledge and rectify his error all around.

Patterson took the whole thing as a good joke, and there the matter dropped between himself and Miss Murdock.

The knowledge that Greene had written to Russell, at New York, and had received a satisfactory reply, was of great value to me, for it gave assurance of my detective's freedom from suspicion under any probable circumstances. That Greene should find it worth while to write such a letter of inquiry was material fit for my use, and I quickly forged it into another link in the chain of evidence showing him to be conscious of guilt, there being no reason for him to become so suspicious and excited, were he not particularly disturbed in his own mind.

I now determined to direct my efforts towards

compelling Greene to believe that Patterson would make a trustworthy and desirable confidant. To this end I had the following letter written at New York and mailed to my detective at Somerset:

"DEAR JIM:—

"Yours received. Glad to hear from you. Thought you were dead; instead of which you are only buried in the great West. Boys all miss you here, and say you ought to come back and that no unpleasantness would result from your turning up now. Sympathize with your humble servant, who has just been subjected to several weeks' retired life on account of Jake Vaughn's blundering. Would like to tell you all about it, but letter-writing is not my *forte*. Had you been here, we could have put our heads together to some purpose. Am glad to learn you have chanced into such a pleasant place. Are you really going to settle down and become one of the 'leading citizens?' Nothing going on in Wall street. Nothing going on anywhere. Weather intolerably hot, and everybody out of town. Only about a million left here. My best hold, as always in the summer, is in the beer-gardens with 'wine, women and song.' I'll wager that makes you wish yourself back. Write when you feel like it, to

"Yours faithfully, FRED MITCHELL."

4

My design was to have this letter fall into Frank Sloane's hands, in confident expectation that he would communicate to Greene the spirit of its contents, and I instructed Patterson to carry out this purpose in any way that might be most convenient.

An opportunity was soon presented.

The Sunday following Patterson's receipt of the letter, knowing that Frank Sloane would call, he placed it on the mantel in his room with some other papers, but so exposed as to attract notice. Then, when Frank came, he excused himself on some slight pretext, and remained away long enough to admit of the reading the letter many times over ; long enough, as he intended, to induce his guest to cast about for something to occupy his attention. He then returned hurriedly, walked directly to the mantel, and seizing the Mitchell letter, placed it nervously in his pocket, exclaiming in a tone of relief :

"Ah, here it is ! I feared I had dropped a letter on the street, or somewhere."

"Is it important ?" inquired Sloane. "If so, I would recommend you not to leave it lying about the room here."

" Why ? don't you think yourself a safe man to be left in possession ?" Patterson retorted pleasantly.

Young Sloane reddened for an instant, but answered boldly:

"Not if I had any object in being curious. I don't suppose it makes any difference between us, though. I was thinking of servants and people about the hotel."

Patterson felt very well satisfied from Frank's expressions and manners that the scheme had worked admirably, and so reported to the Agency. He also advised me that he had, under a complete disguise, seen the man, Powers, and had sounded him thoroughly on the Hennessy matter, until convinced that there was nothing in it beyond jail-bird deviltry.

It seemed to me that the case was now in a favorable shape for putting into operation a certain plan long since devised in accordance with my promise to Mr. Somers.

I therefore wrote that gentleman that I should be glad to have a sort of brief historical sketch of as many of the residents of Somerset, as, in his opinion, would be likely to answer an astrologer's advertisement, so far as the information might be gathered without exciting suspicion; that I proposed to insert such an advertisement in the Chicago and Crown City papers, with the intention of inciting Greene to apply to the fortune-teller;

when her answer should be of a character to startle him from his assurance, and move him to seek a confidant for his guilty secret.

The plan I had decided upon against Greene was calculated to make his load of mental trouble doubly burdensome, and, as my detective had now become his particular friend, I felt assured if the former were really guilty, a matter as to which I no longer entertained doubts, we should soon be able to unravel the mystery of the Somerset bank robbery.

After a reasonable delay, Mr. Somers forwarded me a great pile of manuscript which proved to contain all I had asked for and more. I judged as I opened the package that there lay before me a complete biography of every individual in the town—man, woman and child. Nor did a closer inspection much undeceive me. Not only was the present generation sketched with great minuteness, but in many instances family histories were entered upon; old homesteads in the East were described; casualties and memorable incidents varied here and there the story of a life; and, in a word, I found myself in possession of too much material rather than too little. To use a tenth part of what was before me, would be to endanger my scheme by a display of information much too accurate.

With the parcel came a letter from Mr. Somers expressing his hearty approval of the plan and a promise that he would aid me every way in his power; a promise the keeping of which he had certainly forestalled. He had excellent opportunities as an old lawyer of the place, he wrote, for learning about the residents of Somerset and vicinity, and if any one should write to the fortune-teller whose history he had not transmitted, I might send him the name, and he would answer as fully and promptly as possible.

CHAPTER VI.

Madame Romolu and her Wonderful Disclosures.

ONE day, shortly after the incidents related in the previous chapter, Mr. Somers was alone in his office, seated at his desk. An open letter laid before him, at which he occasionally glanced with an amused smile that slowly gave place to a look of deep study. An observer would have readily inferred that the letter embodied a joke with some serious matter, and the inference would have been correct; for the letter was from "Madame Romolu, the world-renowned clairvoyant and astrologer," who "had temporarily left the scene of her extraordinary successes in disclosing past, present and future life—the Continent of Europe—in order to make a hasty tour of the United States."

The wonderful nature of her revelations, and the unvarying correctness of her prophecies, as proven in every case where due time had elapsed to put them to test, placed Madame Romolu at the very head of her profession, and fully accounted for the unrivaled celebrity she had attained. Since her arrival in this country her appearance in the principal eastern cities had created a furore of excitement which still continued to agitate the highest social circles beyond the Alleghanies, while her enforced speedy departure from New York, Boston, Philadelphia, Baltimore and Washington, by reason of the short time she had allotted for her visit in America, had been signaled in each instance with general regret. Her stay in the Garden City would be of the briefest, and those who cared to inquire into what has been, what is, or what shall be, should apply to her without delay.

Such, in part, were the words of an advertise-

ment that appeared simultaneously in all the
Chicago and Crown City papers; and it was a
reply to an application of his own that Mr. Somers
was now studying.

A short time before Mr. Somers had received
a visit at his office from Mr. Evans, the county
sheriff. When they had concluded their business
matters, the lawyer carelessly took up the Chicago
Times, and exclaimed:

" Ho, ho! here's a fortune-teller with money
enough to advertise by the half column. She
must have gulled a good many."

Now Mr. Evans was notoriously superstitious,
much given to necromancy and that sort of thing,
a fact that none could be ignorant of, for he was
continually recounting to his acquaintances the
most marvelous tales of what Madame This, That
or the Other—clairvoyants, of course—had done.
Mr. Somers had played upon this weakness, and
that successfully; for his visitor replied eagerly:

"Read it out, Somers; let's know what she
claims to do."

As Mr. Somers complied, he took pains to
ridicule the advertisement almost line by line, so
that when he had finished the spirit of opposition
was fairly aroused in his companion.

"I'll tell you what, Somers," he exclaimed,
" you don't believe in anything of this kind and I

do, at least, to some extent; for I have known of fortune-tellers who revealed past events which could not possibly have become known to them by the ordinary processes of the mind. I'll tell you what we'll do: both write to this Madame Romolu, and submit our doubt and belief to a practical test."

"Agreed!" cried Somers; "with the understanding, mind you, that we show each other our replies. If it be worth while to write this woman, it must also be worth while to acknowledge her humbuggery!"

The two letters were written there and then, and Mr. Somers was now momentarily expecting Mr. Evans to come in and claim the carrying out of their agreement.

Presently Mr. Evans darted into the office, with an open letter in his hand, and cried: "Somers, this is the greatest thing I ever heard of. Just read that! There are facts stated there not known to a living soul but myself. I say there is no earthly way for accounting for that letter without ascribing to the writer powers of divination!"

"By the by," he continued, without waiting for an answer, "we were to exchange communications. Where's yours?"

"There on the desk," said Somers, demurely.

"I may as well tell you at once that it is quite as extraordinary a document as yours can be. I cannot pretend to understand it. So far as we agreed to make this a test case I must acknowledge that you have the best of me."

Mr. Somers then read aloud Evans' letter, which ran as follows:

"H. B. EVANS, ESQ.,

"SIR: In your nativity your signification and hyleg is D. I find from its aspect to ⊗ that you were born 13°, about six hundred miles eastward from your present address. This would be in western New York or northern Pennsylvania.

"In casting your horoscope I find that your father's signification came to combustion ⊠ when you were about eighteen years of age, at which time I judge your father's death took place. The particulars of his death I cannot from the present figure determine. Your mother, ☐☿, died about five years ago.

"You have been in the army, ⊠. ♐. D. Y, as a private soldier, and have risen successively through two grades, Y. X. 2. An affliction of D indicates that you were wounded about four years ago, — *, in the left breast, near the heart, from the effects of which you have never recovered, D fixed at S, and probably never will, D. S. <.

4*

You are married, D. ⊠, and have three children,
⊠. ♂. 3. Your oldest daughter will marry a man
of property, ♂. L. ˥. Your wife's signification,
☿, coupled with ⊠, in the house of death, is
without translation. You will therefore outlive
her many years.

"I find your past fortunes have been directed
by zodiacal parallels with a grave inclination of ⊼
towards ⊠. ♂. This must arise from a disturb-
ing element in your family relations. ♀.. V. ⊴.
reveals the cause—a fascinating widow. From
V. ⊠, zod. par. 69, I judge that this trouble will
be terminated by her death, which will take place
in the first quarter of 1869.

"Your occupation is of a criminal nature, ⊐:
D, or keeps you in close relationship to crime and
criminals. Probably the latter, because D. L,
shows you will have much success; and D. ˥. ✕,
will acquire considerable fortune, and D. ☉ be
much respected.

"Owing to a slight obscuration of your figure,
I am at present unable to determine the exact
time of your death. Should you wish to be
informed on this point, or any other, personal to
yourself, you must send your photograph according to the requirements of my advertisement.

"÷ | C | — = X,

"Per Yznaga, Sec'y."

"Isn't it marvelous?" said Evans, as the reading ceased.

"I am much perplexed, Evans," said Mr. Somers, with a worried look. "I can't bear to entertain the thought that there are persons who can read my past and future at will; not that I have any occasion to hide my acts from others' knowledge; but if such powers exist, life is at once robbed of all sense of privacy. To tell you the truth, I am but half convinced even now."

"None so blind as those who won't see!" returned Evans. "If proof will convince you, you shall have enough of it before long, I'll warrant. The whole town will be writing Madame Romolu as soon as the contents of these letters become known. Let me have that paper containing her advertisement, please?"

Mr. Somers handed Evans the newspaper, and said: "The same thing appears to be in every day. What are you going to do with it?"

"Circulate the news. It's too good to keep!"

Mr. Evans was as good as his word. Within a week all Somerset seemed to know of Madame Romolu and her wonderful revelations. Others had written her at about the same time that Mr. Evans had done so, and none knew, or cared to inquire, who her first correspondent was. The answers received were all similar in character to

Mr. Evans's—that is, they were all interspersed with unmeaning hieroglyphics, signs of the zodiac, and so on; but containing enough of plain truth to confound the understanding of the stoutest skeptic.

In brief time the extraordinary powers of Madame Romolu became the staple gossip of social circles, and the principal topic among business men throughout the community. The Madame's communications invariably began with: "In your nativity your signification and hyleg is "—so-and-so; any unmeaning figure; and this word "hyleg," was hit upon by the credulous and incredulous alike, and applied to the whole revelation. When friends met on the street, the first question was certain to be:

"Have you received your 'hyleg' yet?"

Should there be a negative answer, the questioner would reply: "What! not written? Just look at this!" Then the "hyleg" would be shown, and another anxious inquirer would be added to the rapidly-increasing number.

The ladies were more sly about it.

Endowed, perhaps, with a greater degree of curiosity and belief in such matters than the ruder sex, they were certainly less willing that their credulity should become known. There was, how-

ever, no disputing the testimony of Madame Romolu's letter-box at Chicago.

There the delicate, angular hand-writing of the
more educated, and the small, cramped characters
of the less skillful of the sex, certainly predomi-
nated over specimens of masculine penmanship.

This circumstance indeed was a source of no
little annoyance to Madame Romolu, mythical
though she were, for Mr. Somers's store of information in great part pertained to the better class of
ladies, and the male sex. In reply to a number of
letters sent back to him that he might supply material for the astrologer's responses, he wrote:

"These are all servant-girls. I think it would
be well for Madame Romolu to intimate that they
had been guilty of some flagrant impropriety,
which will, in all probability, prevent them from
exhibiting their 'hylegs'!"

Just prior to the advent in Chicago of Madame Romolu, Greene and Patterson left town together on an extended tour; Greene to introduce
some reaping-machines, for which his firm had secured the agency, and Patterson, to canvass for a
larger insurance custom. The invitation had sprung
from Greene, and Patterson had gladly accepted
it on the ground that Greene's wide acquaintance
through the region to be visited would help him in

the way of introductions, to say nothing of the pleasure of the companionship.

On the second day of their journey, as they were driving from a country tavern where they had roomed and slept together, Greene suddenly asked Patterson:

"Jim, do you ever dream?"

"Sometimes; why?"

"I don't know," replied Greene, absently. After a moment he said: "I had a very annoying dream last night that startled me from sleep, and kept me awake for hours. Do you believe in dreams?"

"As to their coming true, do you mean?"

"No, but as to the past."

"I should think one could tell for himself about that, couldn't he?"

"Not of necessity; not when he dreams about other people, for instance."

"I have often dreamed what I knew to be true," said Patterson; "but quite as often, what I knew to be false; so I fancy there's no rule governing the matter. In fact, dreams are to the mind what your reaping-machines are to these farmers about here—something that no fellow can understand!"

With this sally, which caused Greene to laugh heartily, the subject was permitted to drop—Pat-

terson not caring to exhibit curiosity as to the
nature of his companion's dream, but resolving to
profit by what he had heard.

During the rest of the trip they slept together
habitually, such an arrangement proving mutually
agreeable. Some days after the foregoing conversation, in the middle of the night, Patterson seized
his companion by the shoulder, and, shaking him
roughly, cried:

"George, George !—what under heaven's the
matter with you ?"

"Eh !—What ?" said Greene, who, to do him
justice, did not always sleep lightly.

"What's the matter with you, I say ? Can't
you keep still and let me go to sleep ?"

"What do you mean ? There's nothing the
matter with me !" retorted Greene, rousing himself.

"Why, man, you've been mumbling to yourself like a veritable jackdaw !"

"Is that so ? What did I say ?" broke in
Greene, now fully awake.

"I couldn't understand the words, but at a
venture I should say they were mostly adjectives,
and pretty strong ones at that !" So saying, Patterson turned away and nestled his head in his
pillow, as if going to sleep.

"If I should begin that again, Jim, wake me

up the first thing, please," said Greene.   "It's a
horrible habit to get into, this talking in one's
sleep !"

"All right," repled Patterson drowsily. "Good
night."

"Good night."

In speaking of this occurrence the next morning, Greene never for a moment questioned that
he had talked in his sleep, but betrayed annoyance that he should be addicted to such a habit,
rather than fear lest he should have made any
compromising disclosures.

The news of Madame Romolu's fame met the
travelers far away from Somerset, and was repeated to them with every variety of comment, as they
pursued their way homeward.   Some indorsed,
many ridiculed, and a few denounced the Madame's
pretensions ; but all agreed that her statements
were marvelously explicit and truthful.

Not an hour after Patterson and Greene had
arrived at Somerset, as my detective was passing
the latter's residence, Mrs. Greene called him into
the house for the purpose, as she jokingly said, of
securing his assistance in a spirited argument over
the Romolu sensation, which she had broached to
her husband as soon as he had returned.

Patterson told her that she had found a poor
ally, as he did not believe in the silly trash any

more than Mr. Greene did. Mrs. Greene became quite excited over the matter, from her husband's ridicule of the Madame's pretensions and her own silly countenance of them, and from this, and subsequent conversation on the same subject, my detective discovered that he was firmly set against any form of superstition, and that it would be a difficult task to induce him to write to Madame Romolu.

While the excitement centering in the Madame was at its height, the community of Somerset was further agitated on the morning following Greene and Patterson's arrival home, by the news that the First National Bank had again been robbed.

Since the first robbery, and pending the erection of a structure of its own, the bank had been removed from Sloane's store, to the second story of a building, the main floor of which was occupied as a drug-store. The bank now had two safes, the larger and stronger of which was kept in the drug-store, the smaller, for use during the day, in the bank's office above. It was the smaller safe that had now been robbed, and this time, as it shortly appeared, by burglars. Powder had been exploded in the lock and the door forced open with a "jimmy," or small crow-bar. The thieves must have met with some disappointment, for the entire amount in the safe was but three hundred dollars. This they had taken, making good their escape.

On learning these facts, which were reported to me by both Mr. Somers and my operative, the former requesting that I should again visit Somerset and undertake to ferret out the criminals, it occurred to me that this robbery was a mere cover for the perpetrators of the preceeding one, and that, whoever the burglars were, they had been set on in some round-about way by the party who had profited so largely on the former occasion.

When I reached Somerset, however, I received a report through Mr. Somers, from Patterson, which convinced me that this supposition was erroneous. On the day after the robbery Patterson had seen two noted "cracksmen," or professional burglars, from New York, prowling about the village, and had taken advantage of the darkness of the night to accost them. One was a big, burly fellow with a forbidding appearance, a broken nose and a cracked voice ; the other, a slim, dandified person with a marble face.

"Haven't I seen you in New York ?" asked Patterson, addressing them both.

"Very likely," answered he of the cracked voice, "we were just speaking about *you*—saying we had seen you before somewhere."

"And you didn't lie about it, either," rejoined

Patterson. " Eight-eighteen " (the street number of a notorious gambling-house in New York), " wasn't it ? I came here to lay off. What are you fellows up to ?"

" Looking for work," said the dandy, significantly.

"The devil you are !" ejaculated Patterson. " This is a mighty poor place for swag. ' The gopher was cracked '* again last night. You better look sharp !"

" What ! did they go through it again ?" said the big man. " We heard it was 'beat' last spring, and thought we'd come on and see if it was easy to ' do,' especially as the 'fly cops' were making it hot for us."

" Come, come !" said Patterson, tapping the speaker familiarly on the shoulder, " don't try to play innocent on me. I'm doing things myself, but on a bigger scale. Keep mum and lay low, that's all I've got to say."

At this point Mr. Somers chanced that way and spoke to Patterson, whereupon the strangers left hastily. Patterson then made known to Mr. Somers the character of his retreating companions, and suggested that they had robbed the bank. Mr. Somers replied that he had not a doubt of it, but it would not be politic to arrest them without

* The bank was robbed.

evidence, particularly as so doing might endanger the greater interests in the main operation.

While Mr. Somers and I were still discussing this affair, Greene entered the office, accompanied by Mr. Patterson. The former recognizing me at once, we shook hands in a friendly way; but Patterson stood aside as if in the presence of a stranger. After the exchange of a few commonplace remarks, Greene observed this, and said:

"I beg your pardon, Jim, I forgot you had not met Mr. Pinkerton when he was here before. Mr. Pinkerton, Mr. Patterson—a particular friend of mine," he said, turning to me.

Talk about the latest robbery was then resumed, all present taking part in it. No mention was made of the strangers whom Patterson had encountered, nor was anything of interest elicited; and I may as well state here that no further trace of the robbers was ever discovered. Pursuit was abandoned on the grounds that if the New York men were the culprits, the cost of their capture might well exceed the amount stolen; that their arrest might endanger Patterson's *incognito*, for he was acting another part for me when these men had seen him in the East; that it was highly improbable that the original robbers had engaged professional burglars from so distant a point as the Empire City ; and, finally, that the New York men were undoubtedly the thieves.

During this visit to Somerset, at a later period, I had a long talk with Mr. Somers about Madame Romolu, and derived no little entertainment from the amusing accounts he gave of the ludicrous discussions to which that mythical dame was daily causing.

"Evans is determined to convert me into a true believer," he said, "and for this reason, I suppose, my office has become a sort of rendezvous for gossip about the matter, until I am fairly overrun with visitors. Skeptics and dupes alike take up the subject with zest, and discourse and argue about ' combustion, signification and hylegs' with the gravity of lawyers before the Supreme Court! I have at times been on the very point of bursting with laughter that would certainly have exposed the game and spoiled everything. To my surprise many of the skeptics have begun arguing the different points soberly and earnestly, and often get the worst of it, while I am compelled to sit by fairly miserable from too much joke!"

Mr. Somers then spoke of his regret that Greene was so obstinately incredulous. It would be impossible, he thought, to get him to take any interest in the matter, and as for his writing to the

Madame, that was out of the question. Following this, Mr. Somers told me that Patterson ridiculed the whole affair constantly and with such
apparent conviction that it was difficult to believe
he was playing a part. This action might serve
to draw him and Greene closer together, but Mr.
Somers held, it also tended to confirm Greene's
unbelief, and so, to defeat the very end in
view.

In reply, I informed Mr. Somers that Patterson was simply obeying my instructions; that his
action was under constant supervision; and so
far, met with my approval. Greene now knew,
or thought he knew, of Patterson's entire concurrence with him on the Romolu subject. In view
of this fact it would not be a hazardous matter
for Patterson, while ridiculing necromancy in
general, to drop a remark or two that would seem
to overthrow his own argument. Should Greene
pick him up on such an occasion, my detective
might be trusted to giving the appearance of being silenced, but not convinced. Such a victory,
apart from tickling Greene's vanity of intellect,
would naturally work upon his mind, creating
doubt and curiosity there, and from this point it
called for but little imagination to foresee Greene
himself inducing Patterson to join him in writing
to Madame Romolu.

"For double-dealing," exclaimed Mr. Somers good-humoredly, "commend me to Mr. Allan Pinkerton. I flatter myself that I can play a fine game with tricky witnesses, but to you I yield the palm. Work out your plans, my dear sir, and I will content myself with approving them!"

CHAPTER VII.

A Criminal Party and an Important Wager.

FOR a fortnight after this visit to Somerset, no reports of interest reached me. My detective continued to act his part satisfactorily, but no opportunity for effective work arose.

In the meantime Madame Romolu's correspondence was increasing daily. Her letter-box was now burdened with queries and remittances— the latter not exactly a burden—from country towns in every direction. The town of Somerset, of course, outstripped all others in furnishing dupes, for there alone was she able to send definite information. The magnitude of her correspondence from this single point threatened to become bothersome; and not only that, but dangerous. Many of those who received answers were writing again for further particulars as to the past, and these, unfortunately, were not forthcoming. Mr. Somers' magnificent store of local biography was giving out, nor were other sources of information at hand. Therefore the Madame's revelations were steadily losing in historical value and gaining in prophetic pretension.

And still Greene did not write.

The "renowned astrologer" might not continue much longer to give forth vague nothings for a valid consideration, without too great a risk of public exposure. Some one would rush into print; the example would find many followers; the press would become aroused; and then what would become of Madame Romolu?

I therefore determined that a final attack should be made upon Greene, and so advised Mr. Somers and Patterson, giving them all needful particulars. At the same time an advertisement appeared in the papers, the substance of which was, that so great had been Madame Romolu's success in the metropolis of the West, that she had decided to postpone her departure for a limited period—a very few days, in fact—and that all those desiring to avail themselves of this last opportunity for securing a marvelous revelation, must send in their applications at the very earliest date possible after having seen said announcement.

It now only remained to apply this last plan to attempt to induce Greene to communicate with the famous astrologer.

One warm midsummer's afternoon several gentlemen were seated in the front part of Sloane's hardware store, in Somerset, chiefly occupied in ordinary village gossip and attempts to keep cool. Among them were Frank Sloane, certainly not so dissipated in appearance as when we first knew him ; George Greene, with more crows'-feet about his eyes than when the reader first made his acquaintance, and with a somewhat worn and troubled look in his face ; Mr. Patterson, who had really become one of Somerset's leading citizens ; Captain Maynard, who has previously been mentioned ; and two gentlemen named Marchand and Oggleton, business neighbors of the Sloanes.

"Boys, I'm dry," said Frank Sloane ; "and this weather makes me steadily dryer. Who says beer ?"

"Whiskey's the thing," said Patterson. "Take your poison in the most condensed form. It saves both time and money !"

"Every man to his taste," said Greene. "I say, any kind of a drink !"

"All right," cried Frank, thrusting his hand in-

to his pocket, and drawing out a coin. "Odd
man out; last man stuck. Show up your nickels,
gentlemen !"

The clink of a half a dozen nickels falling upon
the hard wood floor was still ringing in their
ears when Mr. Somers appeared at the open door,
and immediately exclaimed :

"Ah-ha ! Gambling, eh ? An indictable offense ! Caught in the very act, too ! I should be
untrue to my citizenship, gentlemen, were I to fail
to present the matter to the authorities !"

"Matching pennies for drinks an indictable
offense !" cried young Sloane. "Now, you're a
little too nice, Somers !"

"Only for drinks ?" returned the lawyer ;
"and from the ice-pitcher, too ?" he added, looking everywhere about as if to find something
stronger than water.

"The cheering beverage is to come yet," replied Frank. "These preliminaries, which you
call gambling, are merely for the selection of a
victim, unless you want to cut the knot of our dif-
ficulties and stand treat yourself ?"

"Oh, no ; not I !" said Somers laughingly.

"A pun, and a bad one, too !" exclaimed several voices together. "Now you *are* in for it !"

It was one of the standing jokes of the party
in which Mr. Somers found himself that whoever

perpetrated a pun should "stand treat" at once, and our lawyer friend was probably not ignorant of this, as subsequent events will show.

"Well, boys," said he, "you must be very dry, to call such a reply a pun. But have it so if you will. Shall we adjourn to my office? I have some very fine whiskey there, as you know."

The invitation was unanimously accepted, not by vote, but in a more practical way, for the whole party to a man were a few minutes later making merry in the sanctum of the leading counselor of Somerset.

When a social party gets together, if only one is bent on having what is called a jolly time, the probabilities are great that all the others, whatever their number, will follow his lead. Now both Somers and Patterson were determined to make the most of the occasion in hand, and knowing Greene to be more tractable when drunk than when sober, they were always ready to "fill and fill again," and it is needless to say that they carried the party by storm.

As soon as the drinking came to partake of a rather noisy character, Captain Maynard and Mr. Marchand, with different excuses, left the party, but Oggleton, who was nothing, if not a reveler, remained. He was a man of huge physique, of a red complexion over a puffy face, and was possessed

of what has been called "impudently good health."
Ever ready with a broad smile, whether or not
there was an occasion for one, he would greet the
poorest joke with a loud, boisterous laugh, that
would seem to shake the room in which he was
seated.

The party as it stood now were, with the ex-
ception of Mr. Somers, very good singers, and
were never long together, where it could be done,
without exercising their vocal powers. Therefore,
the production of a second bottle of that "fine old
rye" was hailed by Sloane with the exclamation :

"Come, boys, what shall we sing ?"

"Yes, let's have a song !" shouted Oggleton.

"I move that Oggleton give us the 'Friar of
Orders Grey,' " said Patterson.

"Oh, no," cried Oggleton. "I've sung that
to death ! It's been my stock piece since boyhood.
A quartette's the thing."

"Which reminds me," interruped Sloane, with
a wise look towards the bottle, "that the quart
yet is standing untouched. Let's prepare our
throats with a good drink !"

As the glasses were being filled, Frank sang
them the musical toast : "Here's a health to all
that's fair !"

Oggleton then sang "Simon the Cellarer," in
preference to the "Friar," and this was followed

by one piece and another by the party until their songs were exhausted; which was not until the evening was well advanced and lights had long since been forced upon them.

By this time all were feeling merry and talk-ative, and with the cessation of the singing the town topic, the achievements of Madame Romolu, was taken up.

"Boys, do you know I've got an answer to my letter?" said Oggleton.

"No? Is that so? Let's see it," said Sloane.

"Why not let us hear it?" said Patterson. "We can't all see it at once."

"Yes, read it, bosh and all!" sneered Greene.

"Perhaps, when you've heard it, you'll leave that word 'bosh' out," retorted Oggleton.

"I'll put it in if he don't," broke in Patterson. "I don't claim to know much, but I'd be sorry to admit myself duped by an advertising charlatan!"

"I believe a charlatan," said Mr. Somers, rather warmly, "is one who pretends to do what he cannot. Now, I claim to be as skeptical as any one here, but I am bound to admit that Madame Romolu has done what she claims to be able to do in nearly every instance that has come to my knowledge. Facts are stubborn things, and if we have numbers of them tending directly to one con-clusion they make pretty strong evidence."

"Do you mean to have it understood, Mr. Somers," asked Patterson, in a penetrating manner, "that you, as an intelligent man, believe in any portion of the pretensions of this Madame Romolu ?"

The question was a bold one, but Somers had told Patterson that he might, at any time, attack him without gloves, and without fear as to the result; that he would not permit himself to be taken by surprise while such interests were at stake; and the thing of all others to be avoided was suspicion on Greene's part of collusion between them.

Nor had Mr. Somers overestimated his power of self-control, for without the least show of embarrassment he answered:

"Most assuredly I do. I believe in Madame Romolu just so far as she has proven her claims to belief, and no further. I think it is hardly fair that my intelligence should be challenged for accepting the facts; and I think it particularly foolish in any one to so far believe in their own powers as to dispute the evidence of their senses !"

"Here's to the health of Madame Romolu !" broke in Oggleton, filling his glass and raising it to his lips; "let us hope her life may be spared until the skeptics believe in, and the faithful doubt, her !"

The toast was drank amid a good deal of noise, and then came a second call for the letter. Oggleton drew from his pocket a bulky letter and, with much flourish, tendered the document to Mr. Somers, who said:

"Oh, no; read it yourself. What's the matter? Have you lost your voice?"

"Not entirely," replied Oggleton, with a loud laugh. "I thought your professional eye might detect the secret of this woman's strange power if these strange characters were submitted to you!" and again he laughed in a boisterous, knowing way that did even more to disturb the lawyer's equanimity than had my detective's impudent thrust.

Oggleton then read, through many interruptions and animated comments, the following letter:

"MARK OGGLETON, ESQ.,

"SIR:—In your nativity your signification and hyleg is ♏. The aspects bearing upon this figure describe a man of quick temper, | = ♀, and violent passions | = ♂, fond of horses, hunting, ♑ and festivity, ♐ ⊗.

"Your father and mother are dead, ♏, combust, ☌. Your business is found to lie in the vegetable kingdom, ♈ ☉, and is connected with

wood ♈. You have been in battle, ♎ ♎, (probably the late war) as a non-commissioned officer,
♀ □ ☉ , and was wounded in the right fore-arm
✕ ♀.

"You are a member of a secret society, ✳ ☿,
and hope to gain office in it, ✳ ✕ ☿. This will
be realized.

" ✕ is well dignified, which is a promise of
success in money matters.

" ✕ is also in fixed sign succedent and ♈ ⊐
stationary, showing that the tenor of your life will
be even and your continuance in present occupation long, if not permanent.

"Your sympathetic signification disposes
towards combustion and peregrine, through its
and your own, hyleg, and is reflected by ⋈,
which aspect is serious, if not fatal. To make
this quite clear, I should have your photograph
and that of your lady-love; but, as it is, I can
read that you were plighted to one who disappointed you, and that one is now ill unto death.

" You will live to middle age only, ✕ ⊥ ☿, and
will die of apoplexy ⊓ ✕ ⊏.

$$\div \,|\, C \,|\, - = x$$

          ' Per Yznaga,
                    "Sec'y."

"Now I want to know if sensible men ever

"What do you say, Jim? Shall we write?"

sat and listened to such infernal nonsense?" burst
forth Greene, when the reading was finished.

"How much truth is there in it, anyhow?" inquired Patterson, ironically.

"Well," returned Oggleton, "there's just this
much truth in it: Every intelligible statement the
letter contains is true to my knowledge. That
part of it which concerns another, and about
which I don't care to talk, is true, and, I had
thought, was only known to myself. If you two,
who are so ready with your doubts, don't believe
me, why don't you write yourselves?"

The whiskey-bottle was constantly passing
from hand to hand, and Greene, though not easily
overcome, was considerably affected by what he
had taken. Of the others, Frank Sloane and Oggleton were used to it, and could drink to an unknown extent without showing it, while Patterson
and Somers, having a purpose in view, had done
a good deal more pretending than drinking.
Greene, as has been stated, was more pliant when
under the influence of liquor than at other times,
so that none were surprised when, in answer to
Oggleton, he said:

"Oh, well, I haven't any prejudices about the
matter. I'll write, if Patterson will; just for the
fun of the thing. What do you say, Jim? shall
we write?"

5*

As soon as affairs took this turn, Mr. Somers brought forward ink and paper, and placing them on the table, said: "Come, boys, we shall have some more fun out of this Madame Romolu yet!" nor could he wholly conceal his disappointment when Patterson replied:

"I'm agreeable, if you'll pay my bill. It's your joke, and must bear the expense of it!"

"Hang the expense! Who cares who pays?" ejaculated Greene.

"Then pay Patterson's fee and get even with him by making him show his 'hyleg';" urged Somers slyly.

"Agreed!" exclaimed Greene. "Say, Jim, you can't object to that. I'll pay your fee if you'll show your letter!"

"All right," consented Patterson. "It's silly business, but here goes!" and taking pen and paper the two had soon written and addressed their applications to the famous astrologer.

What with the excitement of this triumph, and perhaps the exceptional indulgence of the occasion, the lawyer's naturally pale face appeared in resplendent hues as he carefully pocketed the precious letters he had expended so much whiskey and craft to obtain; and it may be believed, when opportunity offered, he lost no time in conveying them to the post-office.

With a final round of drinks, and a parting song, the company shortly after broke up, but two of them knowing precisely why they had met, why they had remained so long, and why they had imbibed so freely.

The long-projected scheme had at last borne its first fruit. Now, if Greene were susceptible to mysterious annoyance and fear, as, if guilty, he must be, these emotions could be brought into play and worked upon until trouble from it all should become unbearable, and goad him on to a confidential avowal of his crime.

CHAPTER VIII.

A Visit to Chicago.—A Husband's Jealousy.

I AM fond of the Minstrels because they make me laugh, and when I laugh I am enjoying myself.

With this apology for taking the reader into a crowded theater in midsummer, we will enter one in Chicago to meet those three gentlemen occupy-ing seats in the parquet, whom we at once recog-nize as George Greene, Henry Sloane and Patter-son. They are conversing in half audible whis-pers ; possibly were we near them we might learn of something important to the operation. A little patience, however, and we shall know all ; for, though they have had a wine-dinner, Patterson's memory is none the less retentive.

The banjo-and-bones duet, the rival clog-dancing, the time-honored stump-speech, have succeeded the overture, and had at last given place to the drop-curtain, when our friends left their places and walked up the aisle.

"Why, how do you do, Mr. Pinkerton ? you here ?" exclaimed Greene, pleasantly.

"How do you do, gentlemen ?" I responded. "Yes, I often drop in here, even during the heated term. I find it a pleasant relaxation from business."

"Allow me to make you acquainted with our friend, Mr. Patterson," said Sloane.

"I had that pleasure quite recently in Somerset, if I am not mistaken," said Patterson, extending his hand.

"I remember you very well," I answered.

A few casual remarks about the storm which had arisen during the progress of the play, followed, when the trio, led by Patterson, took their leave.

It seems hardly worth while to have brought the reader so far to hear so uninteresting a talk, but it should be borne in mind that the business of a detective rarely appears on the surface of his actions. This was an instance in point. Two indifferent looking young men, whose dress and manners would mark them as countrymen on a lark, had watched this meeting from a distant part of the parquet, and had instantly left the theater bearing with them mental photographs of Greene and Sloane.

Their instructions were, each to select his man, after this making sure of the parties to whom I spoke, and on no account to lose sight of him so long as he remained in the city.

The party remained in Chicago but two days. During their stay no movement was made by either Greene or Sloane without my knowledge.

I had only learned of the visit of the three to Chicago a few hours before meeting them in the theater. Patterson had unexpectedly appeared at the Agency, and stated that Mr. and Mrs. Sloane and George Greene were at the Sherman House; that Sloane had come to the city partly on business and partly to give his wife a pleasure trip; that Greene had concluded to accompany them at the last moment and had invited him to join them, an invitation that he, of course, quickly accepted; that Mrs. Sloane, fearing the threatening storm, was to remain at the hotel, and that Sloane, Greene and himself were to go to Kelly & Leon's min-strels.

From that time until the visitors set out for Somerset, they were under constant surveillance, as has been stated. Their time was mostly taken up with driving about, stopping and sight-seeing generally. Money was expended with a free hand, Mrs. Sloane receiving presents of small jewelry, a bonnet, shawl and other articles of dress from her quiet, but seemingly devoted, husband. Mr. Sloane excused himself from the others whenever he had any business to transact, but not from my special detective, who discovered the business to be the purchase of a bill of goods for his store, amounting to over a thousand dollars.

As this was the husband's first trip with his wife since their wedding-tour, and as the presents he made her were not extravagant in character, I found nothing in these purchases to excite distrust. The bill of goods he settled for half in cash, and half on time. The transaction was in every way a natural one, the nature of his business sufficiently accounting for his possession of the requisite sum of money, and it was impossible to draw an unfavorable inference from it, or from any of his proceedings, nor was there anything in the action of any of the party, to which suspicion might be attached, though their every act was made known to me.

The result, or rather want of result, of this trip, was disappointing to me. I had expected some effort would be made to convert the plundered bank bonds and other securities into current funds. The bonds which had been stolen could only be disposed of in some large city, and Chicago certainly offered greater opportunities and less risk than any other city in the West. It seemed that if either Greene or Sloane were the guilty party, he would naturally have seized the first good opportunity to rid himself of the bank's property, if only to obtain release from the constant dread of detection which must otherwise disturb him.

Recalling the numberless suspicious facts against Greene; his distrust of every new face at Somerset; his improbable tale concerning the fibers of wood upon the safe-knob; his statement that no one could secretly learn the combination of the safe, which I knew to be false, as I had nearly mastered it myself by seeing it opened but once; his pretended discovery of the bit of metal in the lock of the store door opening upon Willow street, and again, his willful misstatement as to the time such bit of metal was found, when repeating the assumed incident to Mr. Somers and my detective ; the anxiety he showed in impressing both of those persons that the discovery in question proved that the robbery had been committed by professional burglars ; the unusual trouble he took in writing to Russell to assure himself that Patterson was not a detective ; and, finally, the constant talk of being poor, and the borrowing of money from Patterson to clinch that belief in his mind, when neither of them had become sufficiently intimate to warrant taking such a liberty with the other ; they all chimed in together so perfectly consistent with my theory of his guilt, that, every time I would attempt in my own mind to argue against it, my previous conviction would invariably be forced into certainty which no possible doubts in his favor could remove ; and, as the excursion party was speeding back toward Somerset, and I sat in my office revolving the whole matter in my mind, I could only say to myself :

" 'The darkest hour is always just before dawn.' A few more hours and Greene will have received Madame Romolu's letter, and then he *must* show his hand. He is reticent, self-possessed and obstinate, I know ; but if there is any value in my experience, every rogue has his vulnerable point, and, Mr. Greene, give me but time, and I shall yet find yours !"

In Somerset there resided a very wealthy couple named Talcott, with whom, in his association with the best people of the village, my detective soon became acquainted, and at whose house he frequently visited, at the urgent request of both. Patterson was an excellent singer, and so was Mrs. Talcott. Mr. Talcott was not; and as Mr. Talcott was a man that liked music of his wife's performing a good deal better than he liked music which required as fine a looking young fellow as my detective to make it complete with his wife, who was a remarkably handsome young woman and a trifle given to innocent flirtations, the result was that by and by there was rather more discord than harmony created by these visits, which, Patterson learned by careful inquiry, was quite a common occurrence at the residence of the Talcotts when any prepossessing gentleman acquaintance became on intimate terms with the family.

This fact did not lessen the number of my operative's calls at their residence, but he gradually became more careful in his manner and bearing towards both. He grew to be a little less enthusiastic in Mrs. Talcott's presence, and a little more careful to please her husband, which had a somewhat mollifying effect; but he could still see that both had a knowledge of his efforts to be discreet, from an occasional quick look of intelligence from Mrs. Talcott, and a half protest in everything her husband did, or said, at his incivility and boorishness.

One evening he had accompanied that gentleman home at his urgent invitation, and after the current village gossip had been exhausted, Mr. Talcott himself proposed a song.   No sooner had he done so than his wife seated herself at the piano and began upon a little love-ballad into which she seemed to throw a good deal of feeling, and Patterson half surmised it to come, not so much from his presence or any desire on Mrs. Talcott's part to convey any hidden meaning to him, as from the fact of her constant restraint and unhappiness.

In any event her husband evidently placed some unpleasant construction upon her selection and manner of rendering it, for before she had completed the second stanza he interupted her with great roughness and ill-feeling, suggesting in his blunt, insinuating way, that she had abominable taste, or was very forgetful that she was a married woman.

Although Talcott had said this with an affected jestfulness, it was plain to be seen that he was in very bad humor; and the remainder of the evening was passed in a constrained manner, indicating

conclusively that all of the three were greatly em-
barrassed by the circumstance; and Patterson
took his departure soon after, very much chagrined at the turn things had taken.

Such was my detective's acquaintance with the
Talcotts at the time of his leaving Somerset with
Greene and Mr. and Mrs. Sloane, on the occasion of their trip to Chicago. Had not subsequent events made this family of some interest to
me, I should probably never have known so much
about them, for Patterson had merely reported
his visits there as social calls which did much to
establish his position in the community, but
otherwise availed nothing to my purpose.

As Greene had in a measure supplanted Frank
Sloane in Patterson's friendship, he consequently
became more of a companion to the latter in his
visits at the Talcott's; and my detective soon reported that Greene began to express a strong ad-
miration for Mrs. Talcott. In his confidences
with Patterson he would speak in extravagant
terms of her graces and accomplishments, and
wonder how she came to throw herself away upon
such a nonentity as her husband appeared to be;
but he was always careful to use many expressions of respect concerning her, lest Patterson
should joke him regarding this attachment.

The same day that Greene's letter to Madame

Romolu reached the Agency, a short note was also received from Mrs. Talcott, stating that she could not believe in the Madame's reputed powers but wished to test them, as they were the constant theme of conversation among her friends. She wrote that she would like to have some explicit information with regard to herself, the truth of which she alone might know ; that nothing less would carry conviction to her mind, and that many of her acquaintances professed to have replies from her which had been tested in that way.

Mr. Somers for some reason had neglected to forward me a life of the Talcotts, and on the receipt of her letter it became necessary to write him for particulars. Mrs. Talcott was so favorably known and so interesting a resident of Somerset that my distinguished informer was particularly careful in ferreting out her history. When his reply came to hand, which was after some delay, I found myself in possession of many more facts than previously narrated, together with references to Patterson and Greene which proved peculiarly interesting.

But let us now see what Madame Romolu wrote to Greene, and what was its effect.

CHAPTER IX.

Greene's "hyleg."—Defeat threatened.—Despondency of the Bank Officials.

THE next day after the return of our friends from their trip to Chicago, Mr. Somers, Mr. Evans and Dr. Comstock, a prominent physician of Somerset, were seated in the former's office, all smoking, and each occasionally dropping an idle remark, more to divide silence than with a purpose to bring on conversation.

Finally, after a long pause, Evans broke in with: "By the by, Patterson and Green returned last night. I wonder if they have received their answers from Madame Romolu yet?"

"Answers must have come while they were away," said Somers. "I am curious to know what the Madame has to say."

"'Talk of the devil,'" exclaimed Evans, "there's Patterson across the street, and looking as black as a storm-cloud. Something's up."

"Call him over," cried Dr. Comstock. "I understand he was to show his 'hyleg'"

"Yes, that was the understanding, I believe," said Somers. "Greene paid the fee, and Patterson was to show his reply."

A moment later, in response to Evans's call,

Patterson entered the office. His manner was flustered, and a slight scowl showed plainly enough that something had occurred to worry him.

"Where's Greene?" he asked abruptly. "Has any one seen him this morning?"

"He hasn't been here," replied Somers. "What's up?"

"Oh, nothing. I wanted to see him. That's all."

"Have you received your letter yet?" inquired Evans.

"What letter?" rejoined Patterson quickly.

"Why, your 'hyleg,' of course."

"How did you know it had come?"

"I hardly know it yet, but your manner would suggest it, if nothing else," retorted Evans.

As Patterson was about to reply, Greene entered with an excited air, which at once drew the attention of the company. He was very pale; so pale as to suggest some fright, had not his tightly compressed lips and firmly set jaws more strongly indicated anger and determination. Although these evidences of excitedness were plain to all, Greene strove to appear at his ease, saying with forced pleasantry, as he closed the doors behind him:

"Good morning, gentlemen; did you light your cigars with the weather?"

"No," said Somers quickly, "Madame Romolu's letters would answer still better for that purpose, if we may judge by their inflammatory effects!"

"Come, now, let's see your hylegs," broke in Evans. "It's clear enough they are unsatisfactory, and, therefore, probably true and interesting!"

"Yes, let's have the letters!" joined in Dr. Comstock.

"I have no letter to show," said Patterson, doggedly.

"You're bound to show it!" burst forth Somers. "Greene paid your fee with that express understanding."

"If Mr. Greene demands to see it, I have nothing to say," returned Patterson with apparent vexation.

"Make him show it, Greene," exclaimed Evans.

Patterson had refused to show his letter that Greene might be encouraged to a like course, and also because it contained accusations against himself that it would not do to make public, lest they should be believed. He expected that these two letters would soon become a secret between Greene and himself—a secret of such grave importance that the fullest confidences would naturally follow.

This was in accordance with my wishes, although I had at first planned that Greene's reply from Madame Romolu should be addressed to Mr. Patterson, and Patterson's to Greene, leaving it to be inferred that the envelopes had been transposed by mistake; but Patterson had assured me that he could readily induce Greene to show his letter, and suggested that the risk of suspicion, incident to the apparent blunder, was an unnecessary one. Knowing that Patterson was the better judge of his influence over Greene, and satisfied that he was not overestimating it, I thereupon changed my plan and had the letters properly forwarded.

It was then clearly of great importance that Greene should not call upon Patterson to publicly expose his letter. Refusal to comply would be dangerous to my detective's reputation; if he complied, that would prevent the creation of an inviolable secret between them. When, therefore, Evans made his appeal to Greene, Patterson hastily interposed:

"You are not going to make me show what I distinctly object to having made public, are you, George?"

"No, Jim;" answered Greene. "But," he

added after a long pause, and to Patterson's utter
confusion, "there's no good reason why I
shouldn't show mine!"

As he spoke, Greene nervously fumbled in his
pockets and drew forth the document which was
intended to be the means of his own undoing.

In Patterson's report of this scene, he wrote
that he could scarcely conceal his surprise and
disappointment at such action on Greene's part.
He had watched Greene closely from the moment
he appeared in the office, and had seen that he
was using all his will-power to strengthen himself
in some fixed purpose ; but he was altogether un-
prepared to find that purpose was not concealment, but disclosure.

At the moment Patterson fancied the whole
case was proving a failure. Months of arduous
labor, indeed, the very operation itself, seemed to
hinge on Greene's secrecy. And yet the latter
was about to read aloud in public a letter clearly
pointing to him as the robber of the bank—a letter, moreover, that no small proportion of the people of Somerset believed to be written by one endowed with supernatural powers of discerning
truth, as many of the same people do to this
day.

There was nothing to be done for it, however,
but await the result ; so Patterson choked off his

disappointment and listened as complacently as he might to Greene's reading of the following letter:

" GEORGE GREENE, ESQ.,

" SIR : In your nativity your signification and hyleg are ⨯.

" I find that by the placement of your figure you were born 1° East, and 3° South, of your present place of abode, in a very thinly settled country where useful minerals are found, ♅ ♈, in subterranean lakes ♋.

" The aspects to your hyleg describe a married man ⨯ ☾, having three children, ☉ ≡ ⨯, the oldest a boy, ♎, the others, girls ♉. By an evil combustion of your wife's hyleg with its corresponding signification, ☽ comb. ♀, it appears she suffered about one year ago a serious and afflictive illness, □ ⊙.

" You have traveled considerably, ☾ ⨯; have worked at several trades, ⊕ △ ♑, particularly in iron, ⊕ and leather, ♑.

" Your parents are dead, ⨯ ○ ⨯. They had eight children, seven girls ♈ ▫, and one boy, ♎. Four of your children are dead, ⨯ ▫, two are unmarried, ♋ \\, and live where they were born; the remaining one is married and lives 13° to the

East, near a body of water, ⅃, where you have also lived ⋈⅃.

"You are now engaged in a business of agriculture,)(, in which you handle iron and steel, ⊕ ⊗.

"You belong to a secret society. You hold a high position in it, ⚹ dig. 10.

"Your hyleg has recently been strangely disturbed, ⋈. I read that you are in great mental trouble and personal danger. It is caused by a sweeping affliction of your signification accidentally. The aspects to this became perfect, ♄+6☽, when you were about forty years of age, and show that at that time you committed a crime of money, ⚹ ♈ ☽, in a very skillful manner, ☿ ♒, at night, ☾, by which you gained a large sum, ⋈⚹⋇. Your escape from harm was due to a tempory oscillation of ♈, which at that time protected you. This aspect has now separated from your signification, and your hyleg again reveals great tribulation, ♀ ⋈ □ △ ♌, pressed on at the close, by ⋈⚹ ☿. An application of these prognostications in lieu of the abandoned aspects violently affects your horoscope, betokening imminent peril.

"Evolved by this agitation are other aspects that describe a man with full black beard, curly hair, blue eyes, and sharp, penetrating glance.

He is of a very vindictive nature, strong in his resolutions, D+X, and unrelenting in his purposes, D ⊅⊅X, but what he says may be implicitly relied upon. This man is your enemy, D☉⊹X. He knows your crime, and your every act. Even your thoughts are known to him, ♉ DX. Every indication is in his favor, ☾D☋. His friendship is desirable to you. If he remains your enemy, he will crush you ♓.

"A further indication is that his signification is applying to you through the sign, ☋. This foretells an early meeting with him. The figure is especially dignified in the house of prisons, and a verified application through your hyleg as prisoner demonstrates its completeness.

"The baleful square of ⊗ ♃ = ☾ , increased by the extremely violent aspect of ♄, aspected as it is in your horoscope inversely with your safety, is one of the most alarming and hopeless conditions possible, there being neither analysis or synthesis that will correct your signification and the combustion of your hyleg.

"The aspect of the sign, ⊗ ♓ ☿ , as related to the combustion of its hyleg, becomes perfect in 1882, in which year you will die.

"÷|C|−= ✗

"Per Yznaga,

" Sec'y."

The letter was read in a hard, unemotional tone, a slight curling of the lips alone marking the portion which referred to the commission of a crime.

A long pause followed, during which Greene seemed to be struggling for mastery over some powerful impulse. Suddenly he burst out in an angry voice, clinching his fist and grinding his teeth for emphasis :

"I know who has done this thing ; it's that accursed Allan Pinkerton! but, by God! he shall gain nothing by it! George Greene, thank heaven, is yet a match for him, with all his infernal schemes and agents !"

The effect of these agents was electrical. Dr. Comstock and Mr. Evans were startled into the liveliest surprise. They could only interpret Greene's violent demeanor as an admission of guilt. Somers was dismayed. He felt that Greene's suspicions were now so keenly alive it would be forever impossible to gain an advantage over him. The case was hopeless. Patterson was simply astounded. The shock which Greene's willingness to read the letter had given him, was as nothing compared to the blow inflicted by his comments upon it. Here was a man who in their most intimate confidences would avoid the subject of the robbery, and upon whom he had been exercising his best arts in vain for months; here was this man openly proclaiming that detectives were on his track, and that he would outwit them! Making no declaration of his innocence; not caring, apparently, whether he was suspected or not, he yet exhibited the most uncontrollable anger that an attempt should be made to overreach him; as if this were a greater offense than to accuse him of a crime!

His manner, quite as much as his words, implied the admission of guilt, and manner and words together impressed all present alike; Greene, in issuing his defiance, had virtually conceded the truth of Madame Romolu's accusation. With such a man, what could be done?

Was it not probable that he had suspected Patterson from the first? that Greene had in reality been prepared for him at all points? that while my operative was endeavoring to worm himself into the wary merchant's confidence, the latter shrewdly penetrated his real character? But if this was true, it was a good thing to know it. At all events, it was the detective's duty to act out his part consistently to the end, whether the game was up or not.

While these thoughts were running through the detective's mind, Greene continued his invectives against Madame Romolu and every one

concerned, hinting pretty strongly that he knew
one of her agents at least, when Patterson broke
in excitedly :

"I haven't a doubt that Pinkerton is at the
bottom of it ; though it never occurred to me before. Why, it's as plain as day. These nonsen-
sical letters are all the work of some sneaking informer, some cold-blooded detective, some miserable hound, whose business in life is to spy upon
his fellow men and mulct them in their largest
possible sum for not circulating damning lies
about him—lies, mind you, so mixed up with truth
that the devil himself couldn't tell where the one
began and the other ended !"

Patterson spoke with all the fervor of a man
personally outraged, thus giving out a suggestion
of the character of the contents of his own communication, and, possibly, creating a bond of sym-
pathy between himself and Greene.

"It seems to me, Greene," said Dr. Comstock,
soothingly, " that your position was so unfortunate with regard to the bank robbery that you
have become morbidly suspicious of every reference to criminal matters. I wouldn't allow such
stuff to bother me an instant !"

"She doesn't even mention the bank robbery,"
said Somers.

"No, but she hints at it so plainly," said

Greene, shaking the letter violently in his hand, "that there's not a child in Somerset but would say it meant that I robbed the bank!"

"Perhaps so," returned Somers, "but what do you care if it does?"

Greene looked at the speaker intently for an instant, and then said:

"Not a whit! But I'll say this: whoever gives Madame Romolu her information may as well tell her the fortune-telling game won't work with me!

"I don't even think it worth while to follow her up," he resumed, "but if any one will take the trouble to trace her letters to the starting-point, my word for it, he will find himself in the office of Allan Pinkerton!"

"Come, Patterson," said Somers, wishing to create a diversion, as Greene's remarks had cut pretty close to him, "show us your letter now. It can hardly be any worse than Greene's."

Patterson took a letter from his pocket and made a motion as if to hand it to the lawyer. Then he hesitated, seemed to think better of it, glanced rapidly through the document, and returned it to his pocket, saying: "No, I won't do it! It's just about half truth and half a lie. The truth is what you all know about me; the lies are silly when not outrageous—and that's what makes

me think," he broke out suddenly, "that some
one here in town must give the information."

Evans undertook to dispute this, and Greene
engaged him in an argument into which Dr. Comstock and Somers were also drawn. While they
were talking, Patterson slipped out. He hoped
that Greene would try to see him privately, and left
the office to make an opportunity for him to do so.
He was, then, not a little gratified to have Greene
overtake him before he had fairly reached the
street.

"Do you know, Jim," said Greene, "I believe
Somers gives all the Romolu information!"

"I would be willing to agree with you,
George," returned Patterson, "but to tell you
the truth, what I said up there was only a blind.
My letter was nearly all true, and there were some
things in it I shouldn't care to have known—
things that neither Somers nor any one else in
Somerset knows anything about. You must not
lisp a word of this, you understand! I know I
can trust you!"

"I never tell about my own business, Jim,
still less about that of others," answered Greene.
"I fancy I can keep a secret, if any one can.
Some woman scrape, I suppose?"

"Not exactly; but no matter about that. I
6*

want you to keep mum about my letter's being true. That's all."

"That won't be very hard to do. But wasn't it understood that I should see it anyway ?"

"Why, yes, if you take that ground I'm bound to show it. But I'd rather not; not that I doubt you at all, but my idea of keeping a secret is not to tell it."

"All right," replied Greene, "let it pass. We'll say no more about it. Let's have a drink. This thing has put me in a terrible passion !"

True to his habit, as soon as exhilarated by liquor, Greene became quite friendly and talkative. Referring to the Romolu affair, he denounced Somers in the roundest terms, accusing him of being tricky, false and unprincipled generally. Patterson followed this lead, and kept pace with Greene in his tirade against Somers and bringing me in for a good share of abuse as well; and long before they parted, Patterson realized that his hold on Greene's friendship and confidence was strengthened, if anything, by the developments made in the lawyer's office.

His report to me of the foregoing incidents showed him to be terribly discouraged. He could not see that he was accomplishing anything ; did not find that Greene, in his most communicative moods, showed any indication of making him a

confidant regarding the robbery matter ; and worst
of all, did not now know, nor could he assure himself to a certainty, that Greene was the robber.

It must be confessed that I was greatly chagrined by the seeming failure of the Romolu
scheme.   It appeared to be little short of a disaster ; and when a few days after I received a letter
from Somers, detailing the office scene and summing up the affair as a downright failure, I began
to realize that the operation itself was in jeo-
pardy.

I am not at all an obstinate man, although my
friends sometimes say differently, but I certainly
was not disposed to drop Madame Romolu.   My
detective had played his part admirably.   However closely Greene might study Patterson's conduct, he would find in it nothing to create distrust.
Indeed, the more thoroughly it was considered in
every word and act, the more abundant would
appear the proofs of his straightforwardness and
reliability.

In reply to Mr. Somers' letters I therefore
wrote that in my opinion he took much too despondent a view of the misfortune attendant upon
the Romolu scheme ; that many people made a
boast of not believing in clairvoyance, necromancy, and so on, who were really much given to
such weakness, and that I felt justified in claim-

ing Greene as one of these on account of his dream-talk with Patterson some time before.

I then presented the case fully as it appeared to me, summing up all the evidence against Greene, and reaching the conclusion that it would be best for Madame Romolu to retire for the present, as advertised, but be ready to appear again on the scene if occasion required. I advised by all means trying what could be done with Greene through the regard in which he had for Mrs. Talcott, before definitely abandoning the operation, and further, if this means failed, I should like to try a plan, which I had not yet fully matured, for forcing a thorough confidence between Greene and Patterson, and which I would submit at the earliest moment.

"In conclusion," I wrote, "I feel bound to say that you are now as fully informed as myself regarding all the points of the case, and as the final decision between its continuance and abandonment must rest with you, I prefer that you should judge of it only from your own standpoint. I should much regret giving up an operation of this importance and magnitude, until every promising means of success has been exhausted, but I should still more greatly regret pressing the services of the Agency upon you one day beyond your good pleasure.

CHAPTER X.

*A Husband's Apology.—An Application for Divorce Presented.—
A Visit to Troydon.*

MADAME ROMOLU'S reply to Mrs. Talcott's
anxious inquiries was the cause of bringing
about more trouble for the Talcott family, into
which Patterson became involved, and from which
he extricated himself so neatly as to win still
higher estimation in that greatly disturbed and
most unfortunate community.

There had been a picnic in the country several
miles from Somerset, attended by a large number
of the circle in which Patterson moved, and which
he felt it necessary to join, as the Sloanes and
Greene, with their families, were present. This
picnic was to terminate by a dinner at the Talcotts.

During the day Mrs. Talcott showed considerable excitement in her manner, and Patterson's
curiosity concerning the same was at last rewarded
by ascertaining from her that the nature of Madame Romolu's reply, which contained direct references to both Patterson and Greene, was its
cause.

When the party had arrived at her house in
Somerset, she discovered that the letter had been
lost, and made quite a stir about the fact among

her guests. The mystery was cleared up, however, as soon as the party were seated at the dinner-table, when it appeared that Talcott had stolen the letter, for he immediately began a violent abuse of Patterson, charging him with the authorship of the letter, or at least of giving Madame Romolu the information it contained.

My detective bore the offensive language as long as he could, when he arose from the table, and plainly told Talcott that no gentleman would endeavor to right a supposed wrong in the presence of ladies, and concluded by inviting him to at once proceed to his room at the Greyhill, where they could arrange matters without offense to their friends. Talcott immediately accepted his invitation, and followed after Patterson, blind with rage, and apparently ready for any emergency.

Arriving at Patterson's room at the Greyhill, the latter quietly closed the door behind him, locked it, put the key in his pocket, and then surveying his antagonist and assuring himself that he was merely a bellowing coward, coolly told him that all he had to say was that he had nothing at all to do with the authorship of, or the furnishing information for, the letter to his wife, and that unless he instantly gave it to him, apologized for his insults, and then promised to retract to their mutual friends all that he had said derogatory to

"*He immediately began a violent abuse of Patterson.*"

himself, he would then and there whip him within an inch of his life.

Under this rather startling treatment Talcott saw things differently very suddenly, at once gave Patterson the letter, which the latter tore into a hundred pieces, and then, after apologizing to my detective, returned with him to the house, where he made a thorough and complete retraction before the assembled company, after which he passed the entire remainder of the day in impressing on Patterson what a remarkably good fellow he was, and how very much he regretted that the unfortunate misunderstanding should have arisen.

This ending of the affair certainly gave Patterson fresh interest in the eyes of Somerset society, and withdrew forever any suspicion which might have rested upon him of being connected with the Romolu sensation. It also had the effect of drawing Greene closer to him. Greene saw he was no coward, and he also took many occasions to express a kind of savage delight that the husband of the woman he had no business to admire, but did admire, had been terribly humiliated, and that, too, by his most intimate friend; and in this sense the occurrence directly benefited the operation and gave me cause for gratification.

Some important matters requiring my personal

attention took me to New York about this time, and I did not return to Chicago until the latter part of August. During my absence Patterson made some progress with Greene, but otherwise the operation lagged. Wholly satisfied of his guilt, my detective redoubled his efforts to secure some damaging admission. He had no fear of destroying their friendship by permitting Greene to know him as one guilty of some dark transactions in the East. When, therefore, Greene again exhibited curiosity as to the purport of Madame Romolu's letter to him, Patterson sponded.

"George, I make it a rule never to trust anybody with my personal secrets; but somehow I don't feel as though I could be mistaken about you, and I want to ask your opinion as to how this Romolu got the information against me."

As he spoke Patterson cautiously handed Greene his reply from the madame.

"On your word of honor, won't you ever lisp a word of this to a living soul?"

Greene stoutly said that he would not, and took the letter.

"Now," continued Patterson, in a perplexed way, "I have believed with you that Somers is at the bottom of all this; but, confound it! he don't know a word about me except that I came from New York."

"Are these things true, Jim ?" asked Greene, reading the letter with great interest.

"Yes," replied Patterson, laughingly ; "a good deal more than I propose to have known."

"Didn't you ever consult Somers about them as a lawyer ?" persisted Greene.

"I never opened my lips to him or any one else."

"Then all I have to say is, it beats my time," replied Greene, in a wondering way.

Further conversation and discussion showed conclusively that this revelation strongly affected Greene, and made it clearly apparent that the mystery enshrouding the whole affair had struck deeply into his mind and awakened renewed anxiety and disquietude.

While absent from Chicago I had fully matured my plans for compelling Greene to confide in Patterson, but I was not disposed to put them in operation so long as any simpler way gave promise of success ; and as Greene's infatuation for Mrs. Talcott was great, it was certainly worth while to further play upon his mental anxiety long enough to find whether, as a relief to his harassing condition, he might not attempt an escape with the hidden bank funds, and an elopement with the fair Mrs. Talcott at the same time. It would be a doubly happy climax if in winning my case I should save the honor and reputation of an estimable lady.

But the very next advices from Somerset induced me to abandon all hope of success in this direction and convinced me that Greene's relations with this woman were all one-sided.

The information came to my detective and thence to me in the following manner :

One day Greene called at Patterson's office and rushing in excitedly shook hands with him most heartily, exclaiming : "Jim, my dear boy, I want you to do me a favor? Will you?"

"If I can, yes. You knew that much before asking me," replied Patterson.

"Well, that old scoundrel, Somers, and Mrs. Talcott are going down to Walton to-morrow together. Something's up. Now don't say a word, Jim. I know it. I saw her late last evening sneaking out of his office. I've found out since all about their going away together to-morrow."

"Well?" Patterson said inquiringly.

"Well, I want you to go down there, Jim, and just cut the old rascal out altogether. I'll pay all the expenses and do the handsome besides! Come now, will you?"

"All right, George ; I'll manage it so we can

both get revenge out of the sneaking informer. Never mind about the expenses !"

Greene thanked Patterson with the greatest possible heartiness, and went back to his store a happy man. The next day, true to Greene's information, Mr. Somers and Mrs. Talcott departed on the morning train for Walton. My detective was also one of the passengers, and noticed that the couple kept entirely away from each other, as though such course of action had been prearranged.

On reaching Walton Mrs. Talcott, after a hurried conversation with Mr. Somers upon the depot platform, proceeded to the home of a friend, where Patterson immediately followed, saw her, informed her of the whole affair, and bluntly asked her to be as truthful and honest with him.

She frankly told him that she had come there with Somers for the simple purpose of beginning proceedings for a divorce from her husband. This news quite startled Patterson, and he so eloquently opposed the course, that within an hour she had completely altered her mind about it, and had decided to return on the evening train with Patterson.

My detective then hunted up Somers and informed him that he had cheated him of a client, of which, under the circumstances, that lawyer

was perfectly satisfied, and also told him what
prompted him to make the trip. The two then
arranged that Greene should be made to believe
in Patterson's entire success in preventing an illicit meeting between the couple, and in due time
Mrs. Talcott and Patterson arrived in Somerset,
and a high-toned divorce suit was spoiled.

My detective at once found Greene and gave
him an amusing account of the expedition, pretending that their programme had been carried
out, and that Somers was doubtless at that very
moment tearing his hair with rage over the flight
of Mrs. Talcott.

"I managed it," he said, "so that he just
caught a glimpse of us as we drove to the station
—that was the first he knew of my being in Walton !"

Finally Patterson cautioned Greene as to joking
about the affair with any other than Somers,
whom he might plague as much as he pleased, as
the "old reprobate" would be very sure to say
nothing of it himself, for apparent reasons.

Greene was greatly elated by the success of his
scheme to get revenge out of Somers, and was
correspondingly grateful to my operative, showing
his thankfulness in every possible way ; but only
this far was the incident of any use for my purpose. The operation had now been going on

nearly six months, but with no more definite results than the reader has been shown. Although I had nothing to reproach myself with, I could not help feeling greatly chagrined that so much time and money had been spent to so little advantage. I must now play a bolder game. Greene could not be frightened or coaxed into any damaging confession, and the strongest attempt to work upon his fears had only excited his anger. In a word, the efforts already made had proven utterly ineffectual.

An unexplored field remained. Greene prided himself, above all things, on being a practical business man. In time he must dispose of the stolen property. I was certain from his nature that he would not do so until he felt sure of the parties with whom he might deal. I had long foreseen this, and in the Romolu and Mitchell letters to Patterson I had made it appear that he had been guilty of fraudulent transactions, and I had instructed my operative to clinch this belief in his mind; and I now proposed to follow up these intimations in a way to compel Greene not only to put his trust in Patterson, but, to in time make use of him in attempting to dispose of the stolen bank funds.

In the meantime Henry Sloane and his wife had removed from the Murdock residence and

taken a neat cottage not far distant.   As soon as
this was accomplished, Frank Sloane insisted that
Patterson should leave the hotel and occupy the
rooms vacated by the Sloanes.   After considerable urging, this change was made, and his rooms
immediately became the resort of Greene, the
Sloanes, Oggleton and others of the clique, which
made it still more convenient for my detective's
business, and gave a better opportunity for his
carrying out my plans, as Greene was a more frequent visitor upon him than when he resided at
the hotel.

A second letter was now sent Patterson from
New York, purporting to have come from Mitchell, as before.   After a good deal of gossip about
mutual friends who, it was to be seen by the letter,
were not of the best reputation for square-dealing,
the letter concluded :

"I believe, Jim, that the bond affair has entirely blown over, and it would be perfectly safe
for you to show up here.   Still, if you are comfortably fixed where you are, I would advise you
to lay low for a while longer, as these detectives
are the very devil for hanging on.   Wall street
is played out just now, but things are working so
that I may soon get the 'dead-wood' on the boys.
I will give you the wrinkle.   Alex. Chase was

looking after you the other day. He has struck
oil and is in high feather. All the boys would be
glad to see you back. Write once in a while to

"Yours sincerely,

"FRED MITCHELL."

Patterson shrewdly managed to give Greene
an opportunity for reading this letter by leaving
it within easy reach, and then, excusing himself
to replenish the cigars and bottle, leaving the letter lying in such a position that he was certain of
its having been handled, and when sure of that,
he knew it had been read by Greene, for one of
his morbidly suspicious and curious nature could
never have resisted such a temptation.

In addition to this, the same afternoon he had
a long chat with Greene concerning bond and
stock operations, which came up upon Patterson's
making some reference to the contents of this letter, which he pretended to be very anxious to
keep from Greene. In this conversation, which
Greene pursued with the greatest interest, my
operative gave him such information as would
assure almost anybody that Patterson was well
posted in such business transactions, and he also
plainly hinted at being in the possession of large
means, secured chiefly through his knowledge of
how to secure, and dispose of, at a great profit,

bonds and other securities that might chance to
have something wrong about them ; all of which
had a visible effect upon Greene, and seemed to
fill him with a nervous, troubled disquietude, as
though he were debating in his own mind whether
he dare adopt some certain course of action which
he had half decided upon.

This much accomplished, I felt that I might
move against the man fearlessly ; but just as I
was about to put into operation the plans which
I had long been maturing against Greene, Patterson wrote that Henry Sloane was going to attend
the Michigan State Fair at Troydon, and that it
would be an easy matter to draw out an invitation
to accompany him, if I thought it worth while.

The reader will remember that Henry Sloane
had never been entirely relieved from suspicion, but
had been regarded as the one least liable to have
robbed the bank.   I had not therefore considered
it necessary to fix my attention especially upon
him until something should occur to warrant my
doing so.   Patterson had cultivated his acquaintance in a natural way, and had reported with regard to him from time to time that he was an ex-
emplary, quiet person, just such a one as I had
found him on my first visit to Somerset.   Still, I
had early made up my mind that no one of the
three should be allowed to leave town for any

large city without the honor of my detective's company ; and as Patterson had now been in Greene's close companionship for a long time, and it might have attracted Greene's notice, if he were to leave him for a short time, it would further tend to satisfy Greene that Patterson sought his society for no other purpose than good fellowship.

I, therefore, wrote Patterson to go to Troydon with Sloane without fail.

"If you can so manage," I concluded in my instructions, "it is advisable to *seem* to hold back, yielding only to his urgent request ; but have a care not to close the door against yourself in case Sloane should be indifferent, for the one essential thing to do is to accompany him."

CHAPTER XI.

Sales of Suspicious Notes.—A Projected Partnership.

SO well did Patterson carry out these instructions, that one week after their receipt he left Somerset in company with Henry Sloane, the latter having agreed to pay railroad fares for both each way. Patterson had excused himself at first from accepting the invitation on the ground that

7

business would prevent his leaving on the day designated, and Sloane had at once consented to wait over for twenty-four hours, if that would make any difference. Patterson still hesitating, he next offered the inducement that it would cost him nothing for car fare. As was proper, he at once accepted this proposition with right good will.

The secret of this undoubtedly was, that Patterson was everywhere regarded as excellent company. Frank Sloane had gone off to attend the races at a neighboring town, and, of course, Greene could not leave the store. Sloane would have had to go alone if Patterson had been unwilling to accompany him, and this gave the latter every advantage in acting the part mapped out for him.

It was a dull September morning when Harry Sloane and Patterson took seats on top of the stage-coach beside "Good-natured Sam," and started out on their journey; and two hours after they were seated in the cars which were speeding them eastward.

During the ride Patterson made an attempt to draw his companion into conversation about the robbery, working his way around to the subject in, as he thought, a very artful way; but at the first mention of criminal matters Sloane gave himself up to drowsiness, and was soon, or pretended to be, fast asleep.

On reaching Troydon our two friends went direct to the Franklin House, which was kept by a gentleman named Davis, an old friend of Sloane's and a cousin to George Greene. This landlord insisted on regarding them as his own private guests, and distinguished himself in surrounding them with comforts. After supper all three went to the theater, and returning to the hotel several games of billiards with "drinks on the game" carried them into the small hours. An oyster and game supper, with sundry bottles of "Bass's," fittingly closed the night's dissipation, when at a late hour the three separated with rather uncertain gait and considerably thickened speech.

Patterson and Sloane roomed together. Before going to bed my detective observed his companion take from an inside breast-pocket a large roll of bills, which he placed under his pillow. This was done without any apparent attempt at concealment. Patterson thought it better to notice it, as would be natural under the circumstances.

"You seem to be tolerably flush, Harry. Been making a strike?" asked Patterson.

"Oh, they are all small bills, and don't

amount to much," answered Sloane. "I've got
to buy some furniture and a few things here, so I
drew a few hundreds in convenient shape before
starting."

Patterson was somewhat surprised at the par-
ticularity of this answer, and might have pursued
the matter further had not Sloane turned him off
by complaining of a headache, which he attributed
to the evening's excesses, and then prevented
further conversation by going hastily to bed.

I was greatly interested in the report which
brought this incident to my knowledge. Certainly
Patterson's question was put jokingly, and called
for an answer in the same spirit, especially as the
whole evening had been passed in light talk and
frivolity. Sloane's reply was too serious, and was
not altogether direct. He seemed to have answered some question which he thought *might*
be put to him, rather than the one asked. When
further advices came to hand, I learned that the
second day of their stay had been passed in an
uneventful round of pleasure-seeking. In the
morning they drove about the handsome residence
portion of the city; they next visited the State
Fair, where they strolled about until the dinner-
hour; the afternoon was largely given up to billiards, and in the evening they were again at the
theater.

Patterson had made no headway with his companion up to the hour of retiring, and he determined not to go to bed without making a strong effort to introduce the subject of the robbery. When they reached their room, therefore, Patterson ordered a couple bottles of ale for a "nightcap," as he said, and induced Sloane to join him. While drinking their ale, Patterson read from the morning's paper a graphic account of a daring and successful burglary. When he had finished, Sloane dropped some remark about the skillful manner in which the job was done, to which Patterson quickly replied:

"Yes, but they ought to have made a bigger haul, considering the risks they took."

"I don't know," Sloane returned, meditatively. "Three thousand dollars is pretty fair for one night's work, I should say!"

"But there were five of them, that's only six hundred dollars apiece," Patterson persisted. "Just look at the haul those fellows made on the First National last spring—seventy-five thousand dollars!"

"Sixty-six thousand dollars!" said Sloane, as if just having finished casting up a column of figures.

"Call it sixty-six thousand, then," said Patterson; "what's nine thousand, more or less, anyway? I don't suppose there were more than two or three in that affair, do you?"

"I don't know what to think about it; it has always puzzled me," replied Sloane, indifferently.

"You weren't in the town at the time, were you?" persisted Patterson.

"No, I was on a visit to my sister's."

"Isn't it strange that that detective never found out anything about it?" inquired Patterson musingly. "Don't you suppose he suspected anybody?"

"It's pretty hard to say what he suspected. He seemed to be a very sharp fellow. I half agree with Greene that he was in that Romolu business."

"I am inclined to think so, too. Still, he couldn't suspect Greene, could he?"

"You can't tell anything about those infernal detectives. I believe they'd suspect the angel Gabriel, if they couldn't find any one else to fit their theories."

"Madame Romolu put it to Greene pretty strong, didn't she?"

"Yes, but I fancy she gave you something of the same kind. I notice you have never shown your letter."

"Between ourselves," said Patterson, confidentially, "I never show it because there is more

truth in it than I care to have known. The truth
itself wouldn't hurt, but I don't like the Madame's
way of putting it." After a pause, he added:
"If Madame Romolu was one of Pinkerton's
schemes, they couldn't have given up the matter
when they said they did."

"No; I never took much stock in that report.
But confound the robbery! I wish the infernal
safe had been somewhere else. The more I think
of the affair, the more it bothers me; and that's
all the good it does!"

As he spoke, Sloane rose from his chair, and
commenced undressing. It was clear that he
wished to drop the subject, and Patterson dared
not press it further upon him, having already
touched the extreme limit of prudence in his ques-
tioning.

The next day, Sloane early showed a desire to
rid himself of Patterson's presence, and the latter,
taking the hint, went out to the fair-grounds alone.
They met again at dinner, when Sloane volunteered
the remark that he had been busy buying different articles, and, as he was not yet finished, he
would like to have my detective accompany him
in the afternoon.

Patterson assented, and some time after, they
started out together. Sloane bought a number of
presents for his wife, not a few of which were of

an expensive character, yet he never failed to complain that so doing was really more than he could afford. A handsome brooch and ear-rings, a fine shawl, and a set of furs were paid for from the roll of bills which Patterson had noticed two nights before ; nor was it then exhausted.

Sloane, whether on purpose or not, always walked away by himself when taking out his money to make a payment, and it was only by careful maneuvering that my operative was able to catch a glimpse of the roll, and then not well enough to learn the denomination of the bills. When the money was paid in, however, the clerks were not so careful, and Patterson then had no difficulty in discovering that Sloane's idea of "small bills" was liberal enough to cover twenties and even fifties.

Altogether Sloane must have expended over five hundred dollars in Patterson's presence. What he had paid out in the morning could not be ascertained, for Sloane said nothing about it, except that he had bought some parlor furniture, and Patterson, noticing this reserve, had come to the conclusion that it would be imprudent to ask any questions.

At an early hour the next morning the couple left Troydon, and duly reached Somerset without incident worthy of mention.

While they were absent, Somers and Greene met on several occasions, and the result was that their conversations were chiefly concerning Patterson, whom Greene seemed to believe, or at least desired Somers to believe, was not all he professed to be. Greene further confided to Somers the vague hint that he could tell some startling things about my operative should he desire to do so, and always closed these interviews with sharp thrusts at Somers regarding the Walton affair, and Patterson's "cutting him out" on that occasion, which the lawyer bore as meekly as possible under the circumstances.

Mr. Somers seemed to take a despondent view of this fact, and wrote me that he was almost fully convinced that this cautious, suspicious fellow could never be overreached ; but I quieted him on that point by giving him something of an outline of how I felt sure of being able to do it.

When I had received Patterson's full reports of his trip with Sloane, I at once saw that Henry Sloane had been expending more money than his business and income would warrant. The only inference from this was that if George Greene had robbed the bank, Henry Sloane had shared the proceeds of the crime, and that this discovery was the most important yet made.

On the heels of this came a report from Patter-

7*

son that he had received a proposition from Mr. Greene to become a third partner in the hardware business ; he also asked for special and immediate instructions as to his conduct under these peculiar circumstances.

I must confess that this new move was a surprise to me. I could imagine no good reason why Greene should make any such proposition to Patterson unless to again test his honesty, and endeavor to ascertain if he really were possessed of the means which he professed to be. This would agree with the theory that Greene desired to unload some of the bonds stolen from the bank, and wished to assure himself beyond all doubt that Patterson was a man he could trust with so delicate and dangerous a mission. Whatever might be his object, however, I saw at once the necessity of humoring him, and I therefore immediately instructed Patterson to favor the idea, but still hold off sufficiently to prevent the suspicion that this might be the very opportunity desired by him; which would be the case, very probably, were he really a detective. I also perfected arrangements by which, should it appear necessary for him to assume so much responsibility, he could at once close with them and become their partner.

But further reports from Somerset proved that this would be unnecessary.

No sooner did Patterson express a willingness to invest in the hardware business, should an investigation show it to be a desirable venture, than Greene would refer him to Sloane. Whenever my operative approached the latter upon the subject, he would invariably conclude the conversation with the promise that he would "think it over;" and should Sloane show a desire to have the firm's capital increased in the way proposed, Greene would be certain to present some valid objection, so that it was not long before Patterson was able to report that he was certain the two men were playing "fast and loose" with him; upon the receipt of which information I decided to dally with them no longer, but to immediately put in operation a plan which I was certain, if either or both were guilty of the bank robbery, would lead to positive developments.

CHAPTER XII.

A Mysterious Meeting.—An Arrest.—An Offer of Compromise.

ONE evening about two weeks later an October storm had early housed the farming population near the scene of this story. They were now abed, or surely within doors for the night.

No town or village lay nearer than Oakdale from the place where the reader must now accompany me, for it is the silent and lonely shore of Duck Lake, which, in summer, is always an animated resort for Somerset and Oakdale pleasure parties.

Two persons had met here who had evidently chosen the spot for the purpose of secretly performing some very important business, and it was evident that had not the clouds broken away and revealed the moon and stars, they would not have been able to discover the prearranged rendezvous.

"You are late," said the taller and larger man.

"Thanks to the storm!" replied his companion, kicking the mud from his boots.

"I came near missing the place altogether," rejoined the other. "It would have made a bad mess of it!"

"Yes, that's so, as it's pretty hard work to get away from them at all. Of course, you've got the bonds."

"Here they are," said the tall man, taking a package from a small valise, and handing the parcel to the other, who disposed of it in an inner pocket, after which he buttoned his coat carefully about him.

"They're all right?" asked the latter.

"Yes, you needn't count them. I put up the package myself before leaving."

"All right then ; good night !"

With this the nocturnal interview was ended. The larger man took his way towards Oakdale, and his companion trudged off toward Somerset.

The next morning the larger of the two persons who had a mysterious meeting on the muddy shore of Duck Lake the evening previous, arrived at the Greyhill Hotel, Somerset, and registered his name as follows :

Robert R. Marston,

New York.

He then exchanged a casual word with the landlord, and, lighting a cigar, sauntered about the office and into the bar-room. In a few minutes he was joined by Sam, the driver, with whom he had become extremely friendly on the trip up from Oakdale, and who, by way of securing other desired information, he asked to join him in drinking.

In the front of the bar-room were two large windows looking out upon the street, the main street of the place, and between them was a glass door. The windows extended a foot or more beyond the face of the building, and commanded a good view of the most frequented and busiest portion of the town. A small table on which were piled one or two illustrated journals and a few newspapers in fine disorder, occupied the recess of one of these windows, and round about the room were cane-bottomed chairs, much whittled, and bearing the marks of many a village jack-knife.

"Let's sit down, Sam, and take our toddies comfortably," suggested Mr. Marston, taking up his glass and moving towards the table.

Sam followed the example, and drawing chairs for himself and Mr. Marston, they seated themselves at the table.

"This seems to be quite a thriving town, Sam," said Mr. Marston, glancing up at the street.

"Purty fair in that way, sir," replied Sam; "though what ye can see from here is all there is in it, so to spake."

"Here comes something to take your eye, Sam," interrupted Mr. Marston, as a spirited horse driven by a young man, came in sight.

"Frank Sloane's gelding, is it?" exclaimed Sam, turning half round, forgetful that his companion knew nothing of the animal or its owner. "Ah, yes, it's the purtiest specimen of horseflesh a man might see in a day's travel. An' Sloane's jist the bye to own him, I can tell ye!"

From Frank Sloane the chatty driver went on to speak of his brother, Harry, and then of the bank robbery that took place in their store. Mr. Marston asked with some appearance of interest when the robbery occurred, but upon learning it was an affair of over six months' previous, seemed to become indifferent. Sam, however, rattled on, giving a full history of the matter, naming everybody concerned in it, and giving it as his opinion that no one would ever know who did it, for the reason that the detectives had given it up right off, and now so long a time had passed by. Mr. Marston said it was strange they had given it up so soon, when Sam explained that the bank officers wouldn't pay out any money unless the detective would agree to catch the thief.

"Leastwise," he said, "that's what some people say; but there used to be all kinds uv talk about it. I've heerd tell as how the prisident himself might be in it—an' he wid sthamps enough to buy out the whole bank. An' thin, wud ye belave it, some people had it as how Misther Pattherson, a gintleman every inch uv him, was a detective; but——"

"What name did you say?" inquired Mr. Marston.

"Mr. Pattherson," Sam answered. "Perhaps you know him, sir? I ax yer pardon fur havin' mintioned about the detective. No wan wid a grain of common sense ever belaved a word uv it."

"I have some business with a Mr. Patterson in the insurance line here——"

"The very same!" ejaculated Sam; "and shure enough there he stands forninst the window, wid Mr. Greene and Mr. Sloane."

"Ah ?" exclaimed Mr. Marston; "which is Mr. Patterson, please ?"

"The wan wid his back to us."

Mr. Marston quickly left his seat and crossed over to the knot of three persons which Sam had indicated.

"Is this Mr. Patterson ?" he queried, arresting my detective's attention.

"Yes; that is my name."

"Can I see you a moment ?"

"Certainly ;" said Patterson, stepping aside and lending his attention.

"My business is of a private nature," said Mr. Marston, loud enough to be heard by Patterson's companions; "shall we step over to my room in the hotel ?"

"Well," rejoined Patterson hesitatingly, and then added, as if wondering why the stranger could not speak his business out plainly, and turning towards Sloane and Greene, "These are friends of mine;" but seeming to suddenly change his mind, he concluded in a confused way: "Oh, of course, if you desire it!" He then said to his Somerset friends: "Excuse me, boys, I'll be with you again presently."

"No matter," rejoined Greene. "We'll go on to the store."

The party then separated, Mr. Marston and Patterson then entering the Greyhill House, the others walking leisurely towards Sloane's hardware store, which was located about half a block distant, and within sight of the hotel.

Fifteen minutes later, Patterson entered the store, closely accompanied by the stranger. Something unusual must have transpired, for Patterson was very pale. He seemed to be suffering from a degree of agitation which he could not master. Seeing Greene at the further end of the store, he went directly to him. Mr. Marston followed at his heels, as if unwilling to part company even for a moment with his new acquaintance.

"George," said Patterson, in a low voice, "I'm in a little trouble and want to see you. Will you go over to the hotel with me?"

"In a minute," answered Greene, not looking

up from the work in which he was engaged. "What's up? Nothing serious, I hope?"

"I'll tell you about it, George, when we get over there. Don't ask me any questions now, please," Patterson replied, hurriedly.

"All right, I'm ready," said Greene, throwing aside the brush with which he had been marking boxes of goods, and for the first time looking up. "Why, Jim, what's the matter?" he exclaimed, as he noticed Patterson's pale face.

"Oh, nothing! Come along, please."

The three, for Mr. Marston still stuck closely to Patterson, then took their way in silence to the Greyhill House, and to my operative's apartments. These consisted of a sitting-room and a small bed-room ; the two connected by a door, and both rooms opening out into the main hall. As soon as they were within, Patterson said to Mr. Marston, as if asking a favor :

"May I speak with my friend privately in my bedroom?"

"If you wish to leave the door ajar, I haven't any objection," he replied. "Walk right in."

As he spoke, Mr. Marston stepped into the bed-chamber before them, and looked searchingly around. Noticing the door leading into the hall, he turned the key in the lock and placed it in his pocket.

"You must excuse me, sir," he said, turning to Greene, "Mr. Patterson will doubtless explain to you the reason of my precautions."

Greene appeared very much astonished, but said nothing. Mr. Marston then went into the sitting-room, leaving the two friends together.

"George, I'm in a devil of a fix, and that's the long and short of it!" said Patterson, seating himself upon the bed despondently. "This man says he has a warrant for me, and that he proposes to take me off!"

"Whew!" ejaculated Greene, "what's it all for? What are you going to do about it?"

"That's just what I want to ask you. I suppose I might buy him off. But if he finds that I have any money, he may take that and me, too!"

"Buy him off?" exclaimed Greene. "Why, man, of course you must buy him off, if you can. That is——"

"Sh! talk low; he will overhear you!" continued Patterson. "It's all very well to say 'buy him off'; but it will take a deuced big sum to do it!"

"More than you can raise?" asked Greene anxiously.

"No," said Patterson, rising from the bed with a show of courage; "but I don't know what

sort of evidence he has against me. He may be
trying to frighten me."

"Where does he come from, and what is it
for ?"

"It's about a scrape I got into in New York.
He is the superintendent of the Holland Express
Company, and his name is Marston."

"What is the amount ?"

"He wants nine thousand dollars !"

"Is he entitled to it ?" persisted Greene.

"No ; I only got seven thousand out of the
affair," said Patterson, angrily. "He says they
have been at large expense with detectives, and
intend to be paid back every dollar, interest and
all !"

"Take my advice, and settle on the best terms
you can," rejoined Greene. "Put on a bold face,
if you like, but don't be such a fool as to think
of letting him take you off !"

"But suppose it's all a lie !" cried Patterson,
excitedly. "Suppose he has no authority to arrest me ! Come on in. Seeing you has done me
gocd. He must show his papers first, anyhow !"

Patterson then led the way into the other room.
Approaching Mr. Marston, he said in a dogged
way : "You cannot arrest me, sir, without a requisition. You say you have one. I should like to
see it !"

" If you have any doubts on that score," Mr. Marston answered sharply, " I will show it to your friend, here. I don't like to trust it in your hands."

" As you like about that," retorted Patterson. Then, turning to Greene, he asked, " Will you look at it, George, and see that it is all right ?"

"I learn that this man goes by the name of Patterson here," said Mr. Marston, taking Greene aside, "but in New York he calls himself Barnes, and his real name is Davis. You will see that the requisition is made out for Barnes *alias* Davis."

As he spoke, Mr. Marston drew from his pocket a formal requisition from the Governor of New York on the Governor of Michigan, all properly signed and sealed, and bearing every mark of being a genuine official document, for the surrender of the body of one James Barnes *alias* James Davis.

Greene examined the papers, saw that they were what they purported to be, and, crossing over to Patterson, whispered :

" Jim, if you ever traveled under the name of Barnes, I advise you to get out of this scrape at once, no matter what it may cost."

When Patterson saw the formidable document issue from Marston's pocket all his bravado seemed to desert him. His paleness, which had steadily increased from the first, was death-like; and he looked to be on the point of fainting.

"What is the least you will take?" he asked of Marston, in weak, pitiful tones.

"Nine thousand dollars, as I told you," was the curt reply.

"I can't pay it. I shall have to stand trial if you insist upon that amount." Then, with another apparent effort at self-confidence, he continued: "I don't believe you can prove anything against me anyhow. I have five thousand dollars. Will you take that and let me off?"

"No, sir," said Mr. Marston, emphatically; "and, as for standing trial, I have yet to learn how you expect to escape it."

"Can't this matter be arranged *some* way?" interposed Greene. "It seems to me that an amicable settlement is in every way desirable."

"I propose to make no settlement," responded Mr. Marston. "I am here to recover our company's property. If this young man surrenders it voluntarily, he will secure more lenient treatment than if he puts us to further expense and trouble. That's the case in a nut-shell."

"I don't know what sort of evidence you've got against him," said Greene, somewhat nettled, "but this much I do know, he can bring the highest testimonials from this town as to character;

his friends here will help him with money ; and, unless your case is a strong one, you will surely lose by driving him to the wall."

"With regard to the money," returned Marston, quite changed under Greene's earnest indorsement of his friend, "perhaps something might be done. I have no desire to be exacting. If your friend will approach the matter in the right spirit, we may settle that part of it right here. Not to waste words," he concluded, with business-like brevity, "the directors have instructed me to get expense money if I can, but on no account to take less than the amount actually stolen.

"Now," said he, addressing Patterson, "you know just where I stand. You can pay me seven thousand dollars, your share of the plunder ; or you can accept the escort of a sheriff and myself back to New York."

Patterson shuddered at this, and sank into a chair dejectedly, muttering : "This is ruination ! utter ruination !"

Greene drew near, and, placing his hand on Patterson's shoulder in a friendly way, said :

"Disgrace and imprisonment on one side, Jim ; immunity and a clear record on the other. How in the name of sense can you hesitate ?"

"Immunity !" burst forth Patterson ; "there's

just the trouble.　He says he can't settle that.　I
don't care for the money, but it's hard to give it
up and stand trial, too !"

"Aren't you a little hard on my friend ?" said
Greene, addressing Marston.　"I don't see what
inducement there is for him to make restitution !"

"Mr. Patterson, in his excitement, has misap-
prehended what I said," broke in that gentleman,
hastily.　"I simply can't guarantee him against
prosecution by the State ; but if he will act in an
open-handed way with me now, I am willing to
agree that the company shall not appear against
him.　Nor do I seriously anticipate that the State
will take any action, especially as no indictment
has yet been found."

"Have you told any one in town of your
errand here ?" inquired Greene.

"No ; I have spoken but to two persons—a
chatty stage-driver and the landlord.　The driver
only knows that I had business with Mr. Patterson, and the landlord don't know even that
much."

"If the amount you require is paid down, will
you agree that not even a hint about the matter
shall be known here ?" asked Greene.

"I am quite willing to agree to that," said
Marston.

"Done !" cried Patterson, who had been drinking in every word of these remarks. "You shall have the seven thousand dollars, Mr. Marston, just as soon as I can go to my boarding-house and back." And Patterson started for the door.

"One moment, Mr. Patterson, I guess I'll go along," said Marston, with a significant smile. "That will be the better way."

Patterson bowed formally, a shade of annoyance crossing his face as he mumbled his former reply: "As you like, sir." Then, turning to Greene he urged:

"You *must* come along with us, George. I want somebody to witness the transfer, and I can't trust anybody but you!"

Greene nodded his assent, and the trio straightway repaired to Patterson's room.

———•———

CHAPTER XIII.

The Compromise Effected.— The Detective's Antecedents.— A Temporary Absence.

PATTERSON'S first move on reaching his room was to rush to the closet, secure a decanter of whiskey and glasses. Filling the latter for all, and without waiting for the others he gulped down a portion of the liquid, with the re-

8

mark : " 'All's well that ends well !' Now to business, gentlemen." Taking a knife from his pocket, he next seized his valise, and bending over it ripped the lining, saying :

"What I have here is in United States bonds, Mr. Marston ; I presume they will answer as well as money ?"

"Certainly ; if they are all right," was the reply.

Patterson then drew forth six one thousand-dollar bonds. These he handed to Greene, asking him to count them and see that they were correct.

When Greene had satisfied himself on this point he passed them to Mr. Marston, who said :

"There are but six here."

"Great heavens, man, they are at sixteen per cent. premium," exclaimed Patterson excitedly. "Besides, there is over one hundred dollars accrued interest on them. You really get more than we agreed upon."

Mr. Marston thereupon made a minute calculation with pencil and paper. While he was thus engaged, Patterson busied himself with his valise, pinning up the rent he had made. While he was doing so, a few bonds similar to those he had given Mr. Marston, fell upon the floor. This was evidence to Greene that Patterson had given up but a portion of his means after all.

"These are five-twenties of '64, Mr. Patterson," said Marston presently. "I have taken them at fifteen and a half premium—the last price I have seen. I find that with accrued interest the whole sum is seven thousand and twenty-two dollars. The excess will just about pay my fare back to New York."

"The quicker it is so used the better!" said Patterson aside to Greene. Then, hastily addressing Marston, he exclaimed:

"All right, sir. Give me a receipt in full for all claims, and we will not quarrel about the twenty odd dollars."

The receipt was duly written, submitted to Greene's approbation, and accepted; and thus was the negotiation ended.

"I bid you good-day, gentlemen," said Mr. Marston, taking up his hat, "unless"—he added as if it were an after-thought, "you will do me the compliment to join me at the Greyhill bar?"

"Thank you, you'll have to excuse me."

"I shan't refuse," responded Greene with eagerness. He then nodded "good-bye" to Patterson, favoring him with a sly wink that suggested his purpose was to protect the latter's interests, and started off with Mr. Marston.

A few minutes later Mr. Marston and Mr. Greene were comfortably seated in the former's

room, and were well provided with cigars and
other agreeable material from the bar.

It is needless to recount all that was said between these two gentlemen; but Greene's burning curiosity was satisfied beyond measure by
Mr. Marston, who now, that his business had
been so successful, was in a very happy and communicative mood. So on Greene's expressing a
strong desire to learn more of the antecedents and
history of Patterson, the officer related how Patterson was the son of originally very wealthy and
aristocratic parents at the South, who had given
their son every advantage and an excellent educa-
tion; but that at the outbreak of the war he had
joined the Confederate army, and, following its
waning fortunes, had finally become a guerilla,
when his associations had become such as to lead
him gradually but surely into plundering and pil-
lage; that he had also held important relations
to the famous St. Albans' raid; and at the close
of the war, having lost everything, the same as
thousands of others, he became rather regardless
of how he obtained money, so that he secured it.
Knowing all this, however, the Holland Express
Company had employed him on the strength of
his own splendid ability and a professed determination to do better. He had shown marked faith-
fulness and energy for some two years, when both

he, another employee, and fourteen thousand dollars all disappeared together. Patterson's confederate, one McGregor, had been captured, and the company had only been able to secure five thousand dollars from him. Mr. Marston explained that that was the reason of his demand on Patterson for nine thousand dollars.

He also told Greene that Patterson's shrewdness had defied all efforts at his detection, and that his discovery had only occurred through his having been seen in Troydon a few weeks before in company with another gentleman, by a policeman who had formerly been on the New York force and who had been furnished his description. Not desiring to trust detectives again, he had come on to attend to his capture himself.

During this conversation Mr. Marston made frequent reference to Patterson's career in a way that showed Greene that while there was nothing mean, small or tricky about Patterson, that his ability to secure and dispose of stolen bonds and other securities was something remarkable. Marston intimated that he believed Patterson had effected some arrangement with responsible bankers who were above suspicion, and who had connections in Canada and Europe that permitted of their disposing of what Patterson might bring to them in such a way that tracing them was an utter impossibility.

On Greene's stating that Patterson was held in the highest possible estimation in Somerset, Mr. Marston at once gave many incidents showing how generous and kind-hearted he was. He also particularly emphasized the fact that he was never known to give up a friend, or abuse his confidence. On the whole, Mr. Marston seemed to have quite a respect for Patterson's abilities and general good points; and, while condemning his dishonest transactions, gave the impression of his being a splendid fellow, whose close friendship would be very helpful to any person, and particularly any person who might desire the assistance of a man consummately skilled in conducting dangerous negotiations; and, after thanking Marston for his kindness in giving him so full an account of his friend, and again urging him to not mention the matter to any other person in Somerset, which that gentleman solemnly promised to do, Greene took his departure.

A half hour later Patterson entered Mr. Marston's room, carefully closed the door behind him, and bursting into laughter, cried:

"A success! a thorough, complete success! I am here at Greene's request, Mr. Warner, to beg you to leave town at once, so that there may be no possibility of any one's learning of my iniquities!"

Of course the reader long ago saw that the stranger who first appeared on the margin of Duck Lake, and was afterwards introduced as Mr. Marston, of New York, was none other than one of my officers; and that officer was Mr. Warner, Superintendent of my Chicago office, to whom I had intrusted the delicate mission of conducting this conspiracy against Patterson, which had proven to be what he declared it, "a success, a thorough, complete success!" for its object had been to convince Greene, and through him, Sloane, that Patterson really bore the character that he had caused them to believe of him; that he was a fugitive from New York on account of illicit transactions there, and further, that he had special facilities for disposing of his own, and other people's, ill-gotten gains; the expectation being that he might then compel their unreserved confidence. If, then, the chief thing about the plan had been a success, there was no reason why Patterson could not now adopt the boldest measures towards the wily hardware merchants without a fear of giving rise to new suspicions.

The story of Patterson's life, as told to Greene by Superintendent Warner, was concocted at the Agency long before its recital, and Patterson had been advised of all its details by letter. He was now, therefore, in a position to play a fine game with Greene and Sloane, by permitting them to draw from him admissions of what they had learned through Mr. Warner; or Patterson himself might drop remarks, as if unintentionally, which would really agree with what they thought they knew. The reports that reached me for the week immediately following Patterson's mock exposure, were replete with evidences that both Greene and Sloane had been completely hoodwinked. Greene immediately advised Patterson to leave Somerset for a week or two, lest some efforts might be made to rearrest him, in case Mr. Marston should not keep faith with him, and the New York authorities pounce down upon him after he had already been plucked.

Fortunately a little incident occurred just at this time which made this move not only desirable but necessary.

A year previous Patterson had been engaged on an operation for me at Buffalo, where, in the prosecution of his work, he had become closely acquainted with a gentleman named Redmond. This Mr. Redmond now appeared in Somerset, and Patterson chanced to see him entering the hotel; and it was fortunate that he did so, for the consequences would undoubtedly have proven disastrous had Redmond suddenly burst upon him and claimed acquaintance. Through Mr. Somers it was learned that this gentleman intended to remain in the place several days, and both the lawyer and Patterson decided that my detective's absence from, would be preferable to his presence in, Somerset during the period of Redmond's stay, as it would not only avoid an exposure of his true character, but would greatly please and flatter Greene because his friend had acted so readily and promptly upon his advice.

The same evening Patterson met Greene and told him that he had just received a letter from an old friend in Montreal, requesting him to come on to Buffalo without delay and help dispose of some bonds.

"It's a good chance to make back part of what that old scoundrel, Marston, took from me," said Patterson ; "I'm off to-night."

"If I were you, Jim," replied Greene, in a friendly tone, "I wouldn't take any more risks just now."

"Oh, there's no risk in this matter," returned Patterson. "I defy any one to find out my way of getting rid of things. Marston only got ahead of me through that cowardly sneak who was in the Holland Express job with me."

Patterson reached Walton the same evening,

8*

and, on telegraphing to the Agency, secured permission to come to Chicago to remain during the period of Redmond's stay in Somerset.

I was much pleased with the excuse Patterson had invented to account for his sudden departure, for it gave me an opportunity of proceeding against Greene on the same line of attack. I accordingly had Patterson write a very cordial letter to Greene, which I had remailed to the latter by a correspondent in Buffalo. The letter went on to give an account of his trip to, and arrival at Buffalo, and then stated that there was a hitch in his business on account of the non-arrival of his Montreal friend, which might cause his delay a few days longer than intended when he left Somerset, and closed with a request to remember him to Frank, Harry and all good Somerset friends, and the inquiry as to whether the note for fifteen hundred dollars, which had been renewed at Greene's request, had not about fallen due.

In a short time Greene replied in a most friendly vein, expressing an earnest hope that Patterson's "business" would prosper, and that he would be able to return to Somerset without delay. He also wrote that the fifteen hundred dollar note would be promptly met when due.

This money had been loaned Greene partly to secure his friendship, but mostly in the hope that, when due, it would be taken up with bank funds which could be identified. The numbers of a large portion of the stolen seven-thirties and compound-interest notes were in possession of the bank officers. Neither Greene nor Sloane knew this fact, for the reason that it had not been advertised. It was then altogether a matter of chance whether in taking up their note they would use funds that could be traced. Should they do so legal proof of their guilt would not be long forthcoming, and such a fact in my hands could easily be used to extort a full confession from one or the other.

When my detective returned to Somerset, which was immediately after Redmond's departure from the same place, hearty greetings from Greene and the Sloanes were followed by friendly questions as to his doings in Buffalo, that it taxed his ingenuity not a little to answer. In order to have an excuse for pressing the payment of the note, he told Greene that Macdonald, the Montreal party who was to have met him, had quite disappointed him, having written a second letter saying that the bond project would have to be postponed indefinitely, and offering to pay his expenses as a forfeit.

"Then I suppose you'll want the fifteen hundred dollars?" said Greene, on hearing this.

"Yes, if it won't be inconvenient," answered Patterson. "I have some bonds I could sell, but I don't want to eat into my reserve. When is the note due?—I haven't looked."

"To-morrow. Did you put it in the bank?"

"Yes. Still, I can withdraw it if you wish."

"Much obliged; but we might as well pay it now. Harry's just got a sort of dowry from Mrs. Murdock, and we're in funds."

"Something handsome?" asked Patterson curiously.

"Oh, no; only a small sum. The old lady has a little money invested in bonds and so forth, but not enough to speak of."

It now looked very much as if we were on the eve of success, and my detective, with the enthusiasm that this revelation gave, immediately set about informing himself just how much, or rather just how little, truth there was in Greene's statement. To do this, the same evening he secured the company of Miss Nellie Murdock for a long ride into the country, and before the couple had returned to Somerset, Patterson had artfully drawn from the young lady the fact that every dollar which Mrs. Murdock possessed was invested in real estate, that she never was in the possession of any bonds or stocks, and if she had been, she would not have been at all liable to loan it, much less give it, to Mr. Henry Sloane, though the relations between the two were of the kindest.

"Now," thought Patterson, as he sought his room that night, "if they will only pay in some of those compound notes the game will be in our own hands. With all the circumstantial evidence the Agency has, of which they know nothing, Mr. Pinkerton or Mr. Warner will surely be able to break them down at any moment."

But how often that little "if" interferes with the realization of our expectations!

On the next day the note was duly taken up, not with compound-interest notes, but with a certificate of deposit for fifteen hundred dollars, issued by the First National Bank of Chicago, in favor of H. M. Sloane, Esq., of Somerset.

Wonderfully cautious were these hardware merchants. Eight months after the robbery, and yet disposing of their plunder as if it was an affair of yesterday.

Compound-interest notes, it will be remembered by most readers, were a legal tender for their face value, and for many months after their issue were in free circulation as currency. Only when some considerable interest had accrued upon them did they come to be put aside as investments. In this way it came about that they were commonly treated as other current money, and none but the very cautious thought of recording their numbers, as in the case with bonds.

Learning from Patterson by telegraph what kind of payment had been given for the note, I hastened to the First National Bank, in Chicago, where I was well acquainted, and made inquiry as to the origin of the certificate of deposit issued to Sloane. Upon referring to his books, the teller informed me that it had been issued at the request of Messrs. Ryan & Mason, wholesale hardware dealers on Lake street, who had given their check for the same. Repairing to Ryan & Mason's I learned that Sloane had forwarded to them a week previous two thousand dollars in compound interest notes, five hundred dollars and all the accrued interest to be credited to him in current account, and fifteen hundred dollars to be remitted back in a certificate of deposit. Mr. Ryan, whom I saw, informed me that Sloane's reason for sending on these notes was, that he could not dispose of them in Somerset except at an unreasonable discount. Mr. Ryan further told me that they sold the notes to the bankers, Messrs. Norris & Co. To get this information, I was careful to explain to Mr. Ryan, that I was merely endeavoring to trace some lost notes, and that his customer, Mr. Sloane, could in no way be benefited by learning of the same, while he might become so annoyed that he would transfer his custom, by which I easily secured Mr. Ryan's pledge of secrecy.

Going next to the office of Norris & Co., I found to my great discouragement that all hope of tracing these notes must be abandoned. The junior partner remembered their purchase distinctly, but had bought the notes over the counter in the ordinary course of business, and had made no minute of their numbers.

Although this result was greatly to be regretted, it was by no means disheartening. The time had now come when Sloane was seeking to make use of his plunder. I was at least in possession of evidence, thanks to the loan made the firm five months before, insufficient to convict him, but which, used as I knew how to use it, might frighten him into confession and restitution.

But I saw that none but a slow and sure policy would answer; for should Sloane exhibit as much self-reliance and force of character under arrest as he had thus far shown, he might still set us all at defiance. We had, in reality, no proof against him, and with the aid of such counsel as he would certainly call in, if he had the pluck to make a fight of it, he might snap his fingers at justice and retain his plunder.

CHAPTER XIV.

Sloane Disposes of Some Notes.—Another Disappointment.

I NOW sent Patterson minute instructions as to how to proceed with Harry Sloane, all directed to the end that the latter might make use of my detective in attempting to realize upon the bank spoils. The first thing to be done was to bring about a thorough understanding between them as to the purpose and result of Marston's visit. This done, a belief in Patterson's ability to negotiate fraudulent securities, doubtless already established through Greene's confidences with his partner, must be further clinched. Then a trip to some business center, Portville above all others—as my old friend Mr. Race, of the banking firm of Race & Co. stood ready to assist me in any way in his power—was to be brought about, and finally at that city our best resources were to be engaged in bringing about a consummate triumph.

Patterson soon noticed that Sloane, while still exceedingly friendly, began to show considerable reserve towards him. He was pretty certain he knew the reason, and questioned Greene whether he had broken his pledge to him not to reveal the fact of his arrest by Marston. Greene stoutly de-

nied having done so ; when Patterson shortly secured an opportunity to have a real confidential
conversation with Sloane. He came squarely to
business and asked Sloane bluntly if there was
any special cause for his reserve. He promptly
replied that there was not, and went on to say
that he himself had been desiring for some time
to ask Patterson the same question. This point
reached, the ice was broken, and they at once became exceedingly genial and confidential.

Patterson was not long in learning that Greene
had again lied to him. He had told Sloane the
entire story of his arrest and Marston's history of
Patterson's previous criminal career.

This was just what I had desired, and my
operative took good care to follow his instructions
closely and make several trifling corrections to the
story, explaining that Marston was a man who
liked to tell a good story, and would always draw
on his imagination when it was necessary to make
his tale interesting ; and the result was that this
passing estrangement and the subsequent explanations did more than accomplish what had been intended. It not only effected a complete understanding between them that Patterson was a first-
class rascal, but it brought them into a closer and
firmer friendship than ever before.

By early in December the second part of the

instructions referred to had been carried out. Little by little Patterson had communicated to Sloane that a certain firm in Portville had repeatedly bought bonds of him at a moderate concession from market prices ; that whenever he had anything to sell " on the quiet," avoiding all go-betweens, he took it to this firm ; that they asked him no questions and required no guarantees; that he knew nothing of what became of the bonds afterwards, but believed the firm had correspondents to whom they sent securities bought in this country, who forwarded the same to London, where they finally passed through brokers' hands into the strong-boxes of small investment holders.

Sloane had occasionally evinced a passing interest in these matters ; but it was not until Patterson hinted that the Portville banking-firm had connections in Montreal and London, that he took any active part in talk upon the subject.   When this was mentioned a great change was effected. Thereafter he showed but little distaste for criminal matters, and he would now lead the conversation himself, seizing every opportunity to bring it about to the locality of Portville, to the business of banking, and so on to the particular dealings Patterson had had with the firm whose name and location had not yet been mentioned.

Finally Sloane became so anxious on this point that I authorized Patterson to give him the name of Race & Co., previously mentioned. At the same time I gave instructions to have it impressed on Sloane's mind that he, Patterson, was an important personage in the eyes of Race & Co.; one who could obtain from them almost any favor he might wish; and that they gave him very close to the current value of the securities he offered them, while the specially desirable feature of the arrangement with them was, that there was no possibility of any trouble arising from his dealings with them.

I had also forestalled any secret sale of securities to Race & Co. by an arrangement with them that I was to receive immediate information of any attempt by any person from Somerset or any other western town to negotiate the sale of compound-interest notes or bonds in large quantities; for I knew that Sloane's characteristic shrewdness, reserve and caution might lead him at any moment to attempt such a sale on his own responsibility.

All these things being now perfected, it only remained for Patterson to induce Sloane to accompany him to Portville. While this was being brought about carefully and gradually, an unexpected circumstance served to place in my hands additional evidences of Sloane's guilt.

Several of Patterson's lady friends were leaving Somerset on a short excursion to Crown City, and, more to assist in passing the time pleasantly than anything else, he accompanied them on the cars to Oakdale, where they were to take the train for Crown City. After he had seen his friends aboard, from a mere whim he passed through the train, when who should he espy but Harry Sloane.

He had been at Sloane's house the evening previous up to a late hour, and had, as usual, seen him several times during the day. Not one word had been said about leaving town. Yet here was Sloane, seated by himself, a small hand-bag by his side, a fresh novel in his hands, and evidently prepared for a journey of some length.

"Why, Harry! you here?" exclaimed Patterson, in genuine surprise.

"Hello, Jim, is that you? Where are you going?" replied Sloane.

"I just come down to see some of the Somerset girls off, and have got to go right back, as I've got several engagements in the confounded insurance business to-day."

"Well, I'm real sorry, Jim," returned Sloane, with a keen look in his cold, expressionless eyes, "for I should be glad of your company on to Troydon."

The instant Patterson saw Sloane he had made up his mind that by hook or crook he would go with him, whatever his destination ; and this invitation, which he saw Sloane did not mean at all, gave him just the opportunity he sought.

"Much obliged for the invitation," he answered, laughingly, "although it does come after you have learned I can't accept it."

" No, indeed, Jim ; you're wrong. I've some business to transact down at Troydon, and am then coming right back. I wish you could come ; the journey will be confounded dull without you."

"Enough said," returned Patterson, as the train began to move ; " I'll just run back to Somerset and leave matters so I can come, and I'll be along on the next train."

" I'll bet you a bottle of wine you don't," said Sloane, laughingly.

" Done !" cried Patterson, grasping his hand, "and you'll pay for it, too. Good-bye, old fellow."

" Good-bye !" shouted Sloane, and my operative ran to the door, sprang from the train, and gave Sloane a rallying word as the car passed him.

There was no special reason why Patterson

could not have accompanied his friend on the latter's invitation. He had plenty of money for the trip; and his excuse about insurance engagements was the merest sham. But, while Patterson stood talking with Sloane in the car, the latter had taken out his pocket-book to replace some bills he had received in change with his ticket, which was apparently well stuffed with bills larger than the ordinary legal-tender. The back part, in which bills are generally laid at full length and folded in, was not opened, but its ends were so bulged out by a thick roll of soiled greenbacks that Patterson felt certain that he had at last caught a glimpse of the stolen compound interest notes.

For this reason, and no other, did he forge the excuse which would enable him to return to Somerset, secure some bonds with which to make a show himself if occasion required, and inform Mr. Somers of the unexpected condition of things. But all this accomplished, in the early afternoon he was on board the Troydon bound train, just five hours behind his man.

He arrived at Troydon that evening and at once proceeded to the Franklin House, where he found Sloane enjoying himself in company with Mr. Davis, the landlord, and was received by both with many expressions of welcome and friendship.

The evening was passed in a gay round of pleasure, though Sloane refused all drinking on the ground that he had some rather important business to transact the next day, which would require his having a clear head.

Shortly after breakfast the next morning, Sloane showed the same disposition to get rid of my detective's company that he had exhibited on their former trip to Troydon; and accordingly Patterson made a sufficient excuse for his absence to prevent him from feeling that it was intended especially to give him an opportunity.

A half hour later, during which interval Patterson advised the Agency of his movements by telegraph, and of his belief that Sloane had a considerable sum of money with him, he was strolling along Jefferson avenue when he suddenly came upon Sloane and Davis, when the latter invited him to accompany them on their search for an overcoat for Sloane.

There was no civil way of getting out of it, and the three then proceeded to a dealer's nearly opposite the Franklin House. While Sloane was examining and trying on different coats, Patterson studiously kept apart, seemingly interested in watching the passers on the street; but when one had been selected and Sloane was about to pay for it, he left the doorway, and approaching his companions, made some joking remarks concerning the garment, which he concluded by inquiring its price.

" Seventy-five dollars," answered Sloane, holding his open wallet in his hand, and quite unmoved by the questionable compliments his purchase had called forth.

It appeared that the front compartment of the wallet did not contain enough money to meet his bill, and Sloane was compelled to undo the receptacle for notes. Patterson continued to comment on the coat, while the former with evident reluctance, drew forth a one-hundred-dollar compound interest note, and handed it to the salesman. He had withdrawn the note so carefully—sliding it out from one end without lifting the flap, that Patterson was unable to discover the denomination of those below; but were they the same as the one shown, their sum must have reached well into the thousands.

The salesman was not familiar with compound interest. It was near the time of their maturity, and by reason of the large percentage of accrued interest they bore, they had been almost entirely withdrawn from circulation as currency. He took the one tendered him to the proprietor, who pronounced it good. The question of its present value then arose. While Sloane and the proprietor were calculating this, Patterson inquired what was the date of the note, and received it in his hands for reply. In a moment he had made the calculation and given it to Sloane. He had also thoroughly fixed the number in his mind.

Upon settling with the clothier, Sloane and party left the store and proceeded to a jewelry establishment. Here Sloane bought a curiously-carved brooch and a pair of ear-rings, for which he also paid in compound-interest notes. Patterson gave but little attention to this transaction, for fear that persistent officiousness on his part would awaken Sloane's distrust. When it was completed, the party, led by Sloane, started up Jefferson avenue towards the lake. They had gone but a block or two when Sloane turned about and said the shop he wanted to go to must be in the other direction. Coupled with this uncertainty, Sloane exhibited nervousness in many little ways.

Patterson suspected what troubled him, and determined to again leave him for a time, and immediately excused himself on the ground that he had just caught a glimpse of a dashing young lady whom he believed he had seen before, and was away before any further explanations could be called for.

He hastened on until satisfied he was out of Sloane's sight when he crossed to the opposite

9

side of the street and swiftly retraced his way,
coming in view of Sloane just in time to see him
enter McCullom's banking-house on the corner of
Jefferson avenue and Cane street, alone. In the
few minutes which had intervened, Sloane had
rid himself of Davis, also.

Patterson now strolled along leisurely, giving
Sloane what he counted to be sufficient time to
become fairly engaged in whatever business had
taken him there. Then pouncing in upon him,
he rattled away with great rapidity :

"Oh, here you are! I thought you could not
have gone far. That girl was the biggest sell you
ever heard of. Hurry up and get through, if you
want to hear something rich !"

While Patterson was speaking the bank-teller
counted out and handed Sloane a pile of notes,
saying as he did so, in a brief, clerical way :

"Eleven sixty-eight, fifty-four !"

Sloane verified the count, pocketed the money
and walked out with Patterson without a word.
When they had reached the sidewalk he remarked
in a casual way, as if it were an ordinary occurrence :

"An out-of-town customer of ours took up his
paper the other day with compound-interest
notes. That's what brought me on to Troydon."

" Well, Harry," Patterson replied knowingly, "you are not so sharp as I take you to be, if you failed to make something handsome out of the interest. I noticed your wallet was pretty well lined when we were in the clothing-store. But let me tell you what happened !"

"Yes," said Sloane, "how was it that you lost your charmer ?"

Patterson immediately began relating a spicy story of how he had made a huge mistake, and, for his pains, got one of the worst street " cuts " he had ever received, and told of it all in such a humorous way that long before he had finished Sloane was convulsed with laughter and in the best of spirits again.

After dinner Patterson felt anxious to go to the Russell House to learn whether any dispatch had come from the Agency, that being the address he had given. To his surprise he found it as difficult to free himself from Sloane's company as it had been to keep with him in the morning. Sloane made various propositions for killing time, which Patterson one after another rejected, when the former finally said.

" What is your programme, anyway ?" Being satisfied from his manner that something had aroused Sloane's distrust, Patterson answered:

"To be plain with you, Harry, I went back to

Somerset, after leaving you on the train, to get a couple of seven-thirties, thinking I might as well take advantage of the trip to raise the wind. I am going down now to Farrell & Co.'s to sell them ; will you come along ?"

"No, I think not," he replied musingly. "I'll wait here until you come back. But don't be gone long."

Making all speed to the Russell House, Patterson found a dispatch awaiting him, worded as follows:

"Keep your man in Troydon two days, if possible. Answer quickly."

To this he replied :

"Impossible. Return to Somerset to-morrow."

He then went to Farrell & Co.'s, and sold them his seven-thirty bonds. While they were figuring the value, Patterson enployed himself in furtively watching for Sloane, whom he half suspected would follow him. In this he was right, for in a few moments that marvel of incredulity came in view, walking leisurely along, apparently purposeless and unobservant. Leaving the window where he had been standing, Patterson concluded his business at the counter, and went out to meet his suspicious friend, purposely still holding the proceeds of his bonds in his hand.

"Was I long ?" innocently inquired Patterson.

"No," replied Sloane. "I expected you would about have finished your business, and came out to meet you."

Nothing further occurred at Troydon of interest to the reader. In the morning Sloane and Patterson took the return train for Somerset, where they in due time arrived.

As soon as my operative's reports regarding events at Troydon had reached the Agency, I sent another detective to that city to learn, if possible, the numbers of the notes which Sloane had sold at McCullom's bank, but was debarred from making inquiry at the jeweler's where Sloane had expended some money. The proprietor, as Patterson informed me, was intimate with Sloane, and occasionally visited Somerset.

In due time the McCullom numbers were returned to me, the Troydon bankers having been more cautious than the firm with whom we had dealings in Chicago.

But to my utter confusion neither the number furnished by Patterson, nor any one of those given by the Troydon bankers, was to be found among the list forwarded me by Mr. Somers. The only possible solution of this mystery to my mind was, that the notes bearing numbers of which the bank had kept a record, were all together at one or the other end of the stolen packages, and that Sloane had chanced to begin his drafts upon the plunder from the reverse end, that is, from the end where there were notes bearing unrecorded numbers alone.

However this might be it was idle to speculate upon it. The ugly fact still remained that we were little, if any, further advanced in our operation than prior to our trip to Troydon.

———◆———

CHAPTER XV.

The End Approaching.—Another Business Transaction.—Another Disappointment.

IT is the second week in February of a new year. Nearly a twelvemonth has passed since Somerset was startled by the news of the great bank robbery, and still the perpetrators go unwhipped of justice.

For some time after the partial failure of the Troydon journey, a failure in the sense that it had not put me in possession of legal evidence against Sloane, nothing was done; nothing could be done. At that stage of proceedings, verbal admissions would have been of but little value. I needed direct proof of guilt, and this could only be obtained through vigorous measures.

Strategy could not be used against Sloane so long as he remained at home, and to draw him away again at an early day was, as has been suggested, out of the question. When at last the time came that this could be done, Patterson was taken seriously ill with an attack of quinsy. Just as he was on the point of complete recovery, a relapse occurred, which prevented, for several weeks, the prosecution of the work immediately in hand.

Still, save in the matter of expense, the operation itself had not suffered from this enforced inactivity. During the period of his illness, Patterson had received frequent visits from Sloane and Greene. He was thus enabled to keep on the same footing with these partners, in business if not in crime, as before his misfortune. A word slipped in now and then, directed the course of conversation, and that was all that was requisite. It was not to be expected that anything was to be revealed in these sick-room confabs. Sloane and Greene were not to be caught with chaff, nor would they idly give up a secret. Their belief in Patterson had reached that point where they would be willing to tell him all, should occasion arise for so doing, but they were far too reticent to commit themselves without strong provocation; and it was enough that the old condition of things be maintained.

But in good time the second week in February had come, and with it a storm of slush and sleet. Quietly, but persistently and ceaselessly, Patterson had brought about a renewed desire on Sloane's part to again accompany him on another trip of pleasure, and through the half-frozen mud and slush, the stage which conveyed them, and which was well loaded with passengers, made drearily slow time to Oakdale, where the two were to take the eastern-bound train for Portville.

Much planning and corresponding had preceded this journey. It had been arranged that the couple should return by way of Ryan, a large town on the Great Inland Railroad. There they were to be arrested, and Mr. Somers was to be hidden within hearing when the task of breaking down Henry Sloane should be undertaken.

The process of "breaking down" should be explained. It is that of prevailing upon a suspected party, by any persuasions, arguments or threats that may promise to be effective, to make a full avowal of his connection with the crime under investigation.

Patterson had given Sloane to understand that his main purpose in visiting Portville was to dispose of some seven-thirties, presumably obtained in a fraudulent way, and he had a number of these bonds in his possession, which he was prepared to exhibit at the right time. **Messrs. Race & Co.**, of Portville, were advised of Patterson's coming, and that he would offer them some bonds which they were to buy at a slight discount from ruling rates. Two other of my detectives were on their way to Portville with orders to pick up our travelers on arrival, and then to permit no movement of Sloane's to pass unnoted. Superintendent Warner was also speeding to this central point of interest to perfect the understanding with Messrs. Race & Co., and to hold himself in readiness to change our plans should the emergencies of the case require it.

At Troydon, against Patterson's wishes, Sloane insisted upon stopping over night. This delay was telegraphed to the Agency, and thence communicated to Mr. Warner, at Portville, and through him to the detectives in his charge.

The following morning, in Troydon, while Patterson was in the barber shop, Sloane excused himself and disappeared. Hastily escaping from the hair-dresser's attentions, Patterson sought his man everywhere about the hotel unavailingly. He then stationed himself on Jefferson avenue, at a point commanding a view of all the principal banking-offices. Presently Sloane appeared, making his exit from McCullom's bank.

"You're a great chap," said Patterson, re

9*

proachfully, as they met; " why did you slide off
in that fashion? I've been looking everywhere
for you."

"I had some business at McCullom's," Sloane
replied; "but expected to be back before you
were through."

"Selling some more compound-interest notes?"
asked Patterson, airily.

"Yes; I sold four hundred dollars worth of
them; all I had."

There were not to resume their journey until
the next day; so in the afternoon Patterson
secured time to drop in at the bankers, where by
a little careful management he drew out confirmation of Sloane's statement. He did not dare inquire the numbers of the notes Sloane had sold
them, for fear the latter might call again and
learn of it, but these were subsequently secured
by the Agency. As before, they were not such as
could be identified.

The next morning the two travelers left Troydon at an early hour, and arrived at Portville at
nightfall. A light drizzle was falling, and the
street-crossings were ankle deep with slush and
mud. For this reason two commonplace looking
individuals, who followed the Reddell House stage
conveying Sloane and Patterson from the depot,
had rather the less enjoyable part of the journey;

and afterwards, in pacing up and down in front of the hotel doorways, two at least of my employees were tasting the hardships of the detective's life.

Toward nine o'clock Patterson stepped out upon the sidewalk, and said to one of these watchmen:

"We shall not go out to-night. You need not wait. Be on hand at seven in the morning."

"Harry," said Patterson at the breakfast-table, the next day, "I've a good many old friends here in Portville, and I owe a good many complimentary visits, which, if you will excuse me, I will pay the first thing."

A scrap of paper had been slipped into Pattersons's hand as he passed into the dining-room behind Sloane, bearing these words, which he read instantly:

"Mr. Race will meet you here at nine o'clock, to make final arrangements.

"F. WARNER, Superintendent."

"How long will you be gone?" asked Sloane.

"Not more than a couple of hours. Say we meet here at eleven?"

"Very good; I'll be on hand," answered Sloane.

As Patterson hurried from the Reddell House,

leaving Sloane in their room engrossed with the morning paper and enjoying a fine cigar, he said to one of the detectives on duty, idling about the hotel entrance :

"Keep a sharp look-out; he will surely slip out as soon as I am gone."

In Mr. Warner's room at the Globe Hotel Patterson was introduced to Mr. Race, and a long conference was held, the result of which will soon appear.

Sloane and the two detectives were not to be seen on Patterson's return to the Reddell House. Uncertain which way to turn if he should start out, Patterson waited at the hotel, knowing that one or the other of the two operatives would report to him at first opportunity should anything of importance transpire. After considerable delay detective Smith brought word that Sloane was then in a jewelry store on Superior street, in charge of operative Dawson.

At first Patterson resolved to go out and meet Sloane when coming from the jeweler's, as if accidentally ; but recalling that he had displayed some degree of interest in his movements in Troydon, he determined to await his voluntary return. Accordingly, he instructed Smith to continue his watch upon Sloane and to report again in an hour's time if the latter should not return earlier.

All unconcious of Patterson's anxiety and his watchful escort, Sloane made his way leisurely back to the hotel, gazing carelessly into different show-windows, but entering no store after leaving the jeweler's, where, as was subsequently learned, he purchased two handsome bracelets for which he paid one hundred and sixty-five dollars.

"Ah, Harry!" exclaimed Patterson, as he met Sloane in the hotel entrance, "I'm just going to Race & Co.'s. Will you wait here until I come back?"

"Are you going to sell those bonds you spoke of?" inquired Sloane.

"Come along, then," Patterson answered; then lowering his voice, he added: "but, Harry, I trusted one man, that infernal McGregor, of whom I have told you, and you know the result. My experience in that affair makes me timid of everybody. Will you give me your word of honor that you will never lisp a word to a living soul about my business with Race?"

"Of course I will. You don't half know me yet, Jim. It is not in my nature to divulge a secret!"

As they entered the office of Race & Co., bankers, which was but a short distance from the hotel, a gentleman stepped from behind the desks and shook hands with Patterson quietly, saying, in a pleasant, off-hand way :

"Why, how are you, Barnes? I'm glad to see you."

"First rate, Farmer, thank you," answered Patterson. "And how are you?"

"Oh, about the same as ever. Plodding along, picking up my little eighths and quarters now and then. What's the good word?"

"Nothing special," said Patterson. "Allow me to introduce my friend, Mr. Henry Sloane. This is Mr. Farmer, Harry, known to the sign-reading public as the 'Company' of Race & Co. Is Mr. Race in, Farmer?"

"You'll find him in the back office; walk right in," Mr. Farmer replied.

Mr. Farmer led the way in, followed closely by Patterson, and more leisurely by Sloane, who carefully scrutinized everything as if to form an opinion of the house from the character of its appointments.

"Why, Barnes, my boy! how are you?" exclaimed Mr. Race, rising from his desk as Patterson entered. "It's an age since you were here. Give an account of yourself."

Mr. Race was a short, dapper little man, of perhaps fifty years of age. He had clear, grey eyes, and a bright, crisp manner which impressed one with a notion of quick perception and much energy. A keen observer would have estimated him a money-making man, and ascribed the warmth with which he received visitors to habit and policy rather than to natural exuberance of spirits.

"I have been located out west for nearly a year," replied Patterson. "I passed through here some months ago and saw Farmer, but you were out of town."

"Ah, yes; I remember now. He told me about it. Did you go to Montreal when you were east?"

"No; I only got as far as Buffalo."

"Then you haven't seen Mitchell for a long time?"

"Yes," replied Patterson, "I saw him in Buffalo. He came on to meet me."

Mr. Race here glanced at Sloane, who was standing by, and Patterson exclaimed:

"I'm always forgetting myself. Harry, this is Mr. Race;" and turning to the banker he said: "Mr. Sloane is a very particular friend of mine from Somerset, where I am located."

"Pleased to know you, sir," said Mr. Race. "Any friend of Barnes is a friend of mine, if you will allow me to say so. Are you making any stay here ?"

"Only for a day or two," replied Sloane.

A few moments of commonplace chat ensued, when Mr. Race remarked :

"What's up now, Barnes ? I'm sure you've got something you want to sell me above the market ; you never come to see me otherwise."

"And never succeed either," returned Patterson, laughingly. "You have hit the nail on the head, though ; I have some seven-thirties. What are they worth to-day ?"

Mr. Race here referred to a list on file and named the price, saying, under his breath, yet loud enough to be heard by Sloane, "Same terms as heretofore, you know."

"Of course," replied Patterson ; "that's understood."

"What amount have you ?"

"Forty-five hundred dollars."

"All right, Barnes ; Mr. Farmer will fix you out." Then calling that gentleman, who had returned to the front office, he said, "Mr. Barnes has forty-five hundred in seven-thirties, which I have arranged to take of him. Figure them at the exact market-price, will you, and let me have the result."

Patterson took from his pocket a package, and

handed the contents, consisting of five bonds, to
Mr. Farmer, who counted them methodically, one
by one, on the corner of Mr. Race's desk, saying,
"One bond of five hundred, and four of one thousand each. Correct ;" and, calling Patterson's attention to the fact that two of the bonds were of
later date than the others, and therefore bore
less accrued interest, he then made the requisite
calculation and handed the figures to his partner.
Mr. Race made a minute on the piece of paper,
and, returning it to Farmer, said : "Draw him a
check for that amount, will you, please."

"Certainly, if you wish it," said Mr. Farmer,
returning to the front office.

After some delay he reappeared with several
large packages of bills. These he tendered Patterson with a broad smile, saying, "I believe you
will find that correct."

"What under Heaven," exclaimed Patterson,
"do you expect me to do with all that ? Have
you nothing larger ?"

"Sorry to say we haven't."

"Why, man, I can never carry all that. You
will have to do it up in some other shape ;" count-
ing some bills from the top, Patterson continued :
"There, I've taken out a hundred dollars ; that's
all I shall need until I get back to Somerset.

Please do the rest up for me as compactly as you can."

Patterson followed Mr. Farmer behind the counter, and presently returned with a package of waste paper of just the size required for the bills, nicely done up with fresh seals, the wax being yet soft; and it may be as well to explain that the parcel was prepared for the occasion, and that everything was done according to the plans previously referred to.

Mr. Race then talked with Patterson about different persons, asking when he had seen so-and-so and so-and-so last, and giving later accounts of their whereabouts and doings. Patterson would occasionally introduce a name himself, and Mr. Race would, perhaps, have lost all track of the party, or, perhaps, be able to tell all about him.

The New York stock market was then discussed, and Mr. Race said: "You must not hide yourself for the rest of your days in a small country town, Barnes. There will be good active times on 'Change as soon as these cliques get broken up, and then you ought to have a hand in."

As our Somerset friends were about taking leave, Sloane, who had been an attentive listener throughout, said :

"I sometimes have securities to sell, Mr. Race, chiefly compound-interest notes and seven-thirties. In these hard times my customers are now and then driven to settling their accounts with investment securities. It is not at all unlikely I shall find it convenient to do something with you, if agreeable."

"I shall only be too happy," responded Mr. Race with friendly warmth. "Don't fail to give us a call. Ask your friend Barnes about us; he can tell you as to our manner of doing business."

And this was the end of it!

All these preparations had been made, all these expenses had been incurred, and Sloane had simply been feeling his way with a view of marketing his plunder at some future day!

It did seem disheartening, and no mistake.

As the two made their way back to the Reddell House, Sloane spoke of Messrs. Race and Farmer in a very complimentary way, saying that they seemed to be agreeable gentlemen and very nice people with whom to do business; that he liked their prompt way of making settlements; and that if he ever should have anything in their line he would certainly go out of his way to trade with them. Patterson asked him boldly if he had not some more of those **compound-interest** notes. To this he replied that he had not, and that the four hundred dollars sold McCullom were paid into the store the day before they had left Somerset.

Late that afternoon Patterson ran over to the Globe Hotel and apprised Mr. Warner that Sloane had no bonds or notes with him, and that they were to start for home that evening.

Mr. Warner at once telegraphed Mr. Somers, at Ryan, of the frustration of our plans, and also advised me of the state of affairs by wire.

On receiving the news I was chagrined beyond all expression. My first impulse was to order the arrest of Sloane at once. I was heartily sick of dilly-dallying, and believed from all accounts that the man could be far more easily frightened than cajoled. But to break down in an attempt to frighten him, especially in a State from which he could only be taken under a requisition, would be ruinous. After a few moments' reflection, wiser counsel came to me. I determined to await mail advices. With the knowledge I should then have, I could make up my mind what desperate remedies would best apply to this desperate case. I felt satisfied that I could send Sloane to jail and could shake his plunder out of him before doing so.

CHAPTER XVI.

Another Journey.—Unexpected Detention.—Sloane Discloses his Hand.

A GENERAL retreat along the line of my operations now took place. Mr. Somers, in no enviable frame of mind, turned his back on Ryan and hastened homeward, having devoted two days, at no small inconvenience, to say nothing of the expense, to an altogether fruitless errand. I could easily see from the tone of a letter, written immediately upon his arrival at Somerset, and though couched in courteous terms, that his respect for the Agency, and its methods, was weakening beneath the repeated miscarriage of its plans. Nor could I blame him when he demanded more practical results, and referred to the fact that no single scheme had met with any marked success.

Superintendent Warner and operatives Dawson and Smith left the late scene of action together, the first-named gentleman bearing away the forty-five hundred dollars in bonds, which Mr. Race had turned over to him. Sloane and Patterson took the evening train westward, as proposed, stopping at Troydon for a short spree with their friend Davis, and then sped on to Somerset. The only

opportunity offered my detective for the display
of his professional talents on this trip was in the
scrupulous care he was bound to take of his waste
paper, valued at over five thousand dollars. This
he placed carefully under his pillow in the cars at
night, and temporarily gave in charge of the hotel
proprietor, both at the Reddell House, Portville,
and the Franklin House, Troydon, taking a receipt in each instance.

In anticipation of a possible request for a loan
from Sloane, Patterson told him that he thought
very likely he should have to send the whole sum
on to New York as soon as they reached Somerset ; that he noticed by the papers that Erie stocks
had fallen three per cent. within as many days,
and if that sort of thing kept on his brokers
would require more margin, and that he was determined to hold his shares until he could get out
without loss, if he had to send on more than the
five thousand dollars.

Thus, in something more than due course of
railroad travel, all the parties to the Portville
scheme were back at their posts, and I was free to
study up the case at my leisure.

From Patterson's report I soon gathered that
my surmises as to Sloane's object in accompanying
him to Portville were correct. It seemed that before leaving that city, he had paved the way for

his return, by stating that one of his customers who had previously taken up his paper with compound-interest notes, owed him a bill now nearly due, for over a thousand dollars, and the presumption was that it would be settled in the same way.

This information gave me the keenest satisfaction, for it not only approved the policy of caution by which I had been guided, but gave high promise of the early and entire success of the operation itself. The conclusion was irresistible that Sloane contemplated disposing of the bank's property through Messrs. Race & Co., and that, too, at no distant day. It would, then, only be necessary to put in force again the plan which had just proven unsuccessful, and all would be well. Sloane would be arrested with a greater amount of booty on his person, and with such a hold upon him, I should be unworthy of my calling if I failed to wrench from him every stolen dollar still in his possession.

I therefore directed Patterson to bring about another trip to Portville, suggesting that it would only be necessary to fall in with hints thrown out by Sloane, and that it might be well to show reluctance to undertaking the journey if this could be done without endangering the accomplishment of our purpose. This may seem like excessive pre-

caution, but I am never afraid on that side, until
the time for action comes.

We were moving now in the right direction,
beyond all doubt, for even while these instructions were on the way, Patterson reported that
Sloane wished him to go to Portville again.

The manner in which Sloane broached the subject to my detective amused me not a little, as it
was so characteristic of the man. It seemed impossible for him to desert his cunning. Believing
Patterson to be a sincere friend, and having proof
that he was a rogue, as well as a very shrewd one,
he still pretended to wear the garb of honesty
himself. He had used and sold compound-interest
notes in Patterson's presence, offering an explanation too shallow to be believed ; he had made
purchases while in my operative's company altogether too extravagant for his income; he had
half admitted his guilt in many lesser ways ; and
yet he kept up the sham by telling Patterson that
he had been disappointed with regard to the maturing bill of which he had spoken, and wanted to
borrow a thousand dollars !

The last of the bonds which Patterson had re-
tained in his possession from the time of his mock
arrest by Mr. Warner, *alias* Marston, at Somerset, had been returned to the Agency through
Messrs. Race & Co. ; and as it might be necessary

to make another show of a sale to that firm, he now provided himself with a large envelope, in which were sealed some documentary papers, and which he labeled " $2,000, U. S. 7-30 Bonds." The story he had told about New York brokers requiring margins, promised to serve him in good stead at this time. It enabled him to keep up the fiction of intending to lend the thousand dollars, and also furnished him, as he thought, with a good excuse for not doing so when the proper time came.

As soon as Patterson had assented to Sloane's invitation, Greene, who had been brought into consultation from the time the journey was first proposed, urged their speedy departure with a good deal of persistence, and advised that they should start at night, and make the journey with all possible expedition, so that their absence from town might remain unnoticed. He would let it be understood, he said, by those who made inquiries, that they had gone to Cincinnati on a spree, and they must support this impression on their return. No explanation was given by either Greene or Sloane as to the necessity for this secrecy and deception ; but if the story of their crime had been written down in black and white, it could have added but little to Patterson's knowledge of the motives which prompted them.

10

Greene's anxiety to get them off, seconded as
it was by some pressure from Sloane, forced Patterson to set out before our arrangements were
complete. Ordinarily, this would be a most
hazardous thing to do. It is a matter of the greatest importance in all detective enterprises that
each operative should know just the extent and
limitation of his duties. But, in this instance,
customary precautions could be dispensed with,
since it was an old play that was about to be re-
enacted, and one that required no rehearsal.

On a Thursday evening, Patterson and Sloane
took their departure from Somerset bound for
Portville. They were to take the Great Northern
Railroad to Troydon, and thence the Through
Valley and Portville roads to their destination.
Twelve hours later, Superintendent Warner and
detective Wright left Chicago by the Great Inland
Railroad, bound for Portville direct.

On the arrival of the latter two at half past one
in the morning at Elliott, a large city on Lake
Erie, between Troydon and Portville, they were
informed that the track of the Portville road had
been washed away by a freshet at a point some
thirty miles distant, and that no trains would
leave for the east until noon of the same day, by
which time, it was expected, the damage would
be repaired. Upon inquiry, Mr. Warner learned

that it was possible for Sloane and Patterson to have gone through by making direct connections at Troydon ; otherwise they must also be delayed. Thereupon detective Wright searched the registers of all the prominent hotels of the city, but found no trace of the travelers. Under no little anxiety lest an accidental meeting should take place, Mr. Warner took a room for himself and Wright at the Whipple House, and retired, giving orders to be called at nine o'clock.

In the meantime, the Somerset party had reached Troydon, and were tarrying there until through travel should be re-established. An accident to a freight train at Wayne Junction had detained them en route. On their arrival at Troydon they were met with news of the mishap on the Portville road. As nothing would be gained by pressing on to Elliott, they concluded to pass their spare time in the "City of the Straits," as Troydon is called, with their congenial friend, Davis.

Before leaving the hotel to take the cars for Portville, Mr. Warner sent detective Wright to the depot to watch the incoming train from Troydon, with instructions to report to him at once if Sloane and Patterson were aboard. Wright had never seen Patterson and would have to trust to description to recognize his party. This was one of the inconveniences arising from our necessarily hasty action. Had the Agency been able to make full preparation, a detective acquainted with Patterson would have accompanied Mr. Warner. As it was, I was compelled to make use of the first employee at hand, and this happened to be detective Wright.

Mr. Warner, however, furnished Wright with a very complete description of both parties, save as to clothing, and so, felt quite satisfied, when word was brought that neither Patterson or Sloane were on the train, and that the coast was clear. But to be doubly sure, before entering the eastward-bound train, and just prior to starting, Mr. Warner sent Wright through the cars on a second search. This was attended with like result. Patterson and Sloane were not to be seen.

A good detective should be a man of iron nerve, prepared for every emergency, and equal to the requirements of any unforeseen developments. Superintendent Warner had perhaps as good a title to these qualifications as any man in my employ ; and yet, when after being in the cars a few minutes he looked up from his paper and saw Harry Sloane, not ten feet distant, gazing him steadily in the face, he felt himself grow hot and cold by turns, and was startled to the very verge of an outburst. In his report of the occurrence, he said:

"My heart fairly leaped into my mouth. The issues at stake were so great, the disaster attending a false move would be so complete and overwhelming, that I trembled with anxiety in spite of myself. The wild thought came to me of arresting him on the spot, and I do not know but I should have done so, had he in any way shown he recognized me ; but he simply fixed his expressionless eyes upon me, and I could no more read what was going on in his mind than if he were a statue."

His suspense lasted but a moment. The watchful Patterson took in the situation at a glance, and drew Sloane's attention by an animated story, requiring in its recital many gestures and much laughter. At the first way station, to Mr. Warner's infinite relief, they left the car. The next moment Patterson was at his side saying, "I am not sure, but I hardly think he has recognized you. Remain where you are. I will take him into the baggage-car and keep him there until we reach Portville."

This programme Patterson was fortunately able to carry out. Before the train was at a stand-still at Portville, Mr. Warner and detective Wright had jumped from the cars, and were out of sight on their way to the Globe Hotel.

"Harry," said Patterson to Sloane, as they left the cars, "take a good look at that lady ahead, will you, and tell me whether you know her?"

"Which one?" inquired Sloane; "there are a hundred of them."

"The one in a brown traveling-dress with that man carrying a valise—there! They've just stopped to engage a cab. Look around as we pass them."

"Well?" queried Sloane, having done as my operative requested.

"Do you know her?" asked Patterson.

"No."

"Are you sure, Sloane? I saw her in the cars, and I have been puzzling my brains ever since to recall where I have met her. I'm certain I have seen her somewhere, and that not long ago, too. Confound it!" he broke out, petulantly, "how annoying it is to encounter familiar faces and not be able to replace them."

"I am not troubled in that way," said Sloane. "Names sometimes escape me, but I never forget faces."

"And I," rejoined Patterson, "rarely ride in the cars without meeting some one whose face is familiar, yet whose identity I can't be certain of. It's very annoying."

"I presume it's only the female faces that trouble you that way," said Sloane, dryly.

"You are wrong there, Harry. On this very train, just as we got aboard at Elliott, I caught a glimpse of a man whom I could swear I had seen in Somerset. Did you notice any one?"

"Not I," answered Sloane.

"I'll tell you what it is, Jim," Sloane added, confidentially, "you are allowing your private matters to prey upon your fears. I thought you were a man of more grit."

On reaching the Reddell House Patterson took the first opportunity to run over to the Globe Hotel and inform Mr. Warner of the happy issue of the incident on the cars, which was a piece of strange good fortune, considering Sloane's boast of such a retentive memory for faces. An interview was arranged for that evening at nine o'clock in Mr. Warner's room, and detective Wright was sent to invite Mr. Race to be present in order that there might be no hitch in the arrangements for Monday. Upon that operative's return, he repaired to the vicinity of the Reddell House, with instructions to not allow Sloane to escape his sight save when in bed, while he remained in Portville.

Notwithstanding his engagement for nine o'clock, Patterson found it impossible to resist Sloane's importunities for his company to the theater, and to the theater they went. Patterson's throat still troubled him slightly. At an exciting point of the play he made this an excuse to go out and treat it with a gargle, saying, as he left, that if that should not relieve him he would consult a physician, but in any case he would be back before the play was over.

With a parting caution to Wright, who was on duty outside of the theater, Patterson darted over to the Globe Hotel and arranged with Mr. Race and Mr. Warner the details of another mock sale of bonds. As he was about taking his leave, Patterson said to Mr. Warner:

"I have partly agreed to lend Sloane a thousand dollars. If he should ask me for it when Mr. Farmer hands me the money, I shall tell him my brokers in New York require more margin. Will that be sufficient excuse, do you think ?"

"No, that won't do ;" replied Mr. Warner. "You have told him you are interested in a rise in 'Erie'; now if 'Erie' should happen to be higher on Monday, where would be your excuse ? No ; we must manage better than that."

"'Erie' has risen two per cent. to-day," broke in Mr. Race. "That ought to settle that matter."

"I will have a telegram sent from your friend, Mitchell," said Mr. Warner. "He will be arrested and have to give bonds. The telegram will be addressed to you, care of Race & Co., and Mr. Farmer, if Mr. Race will so direct, will give it to you as soon as you enter the office. Sloane already knows that Mitchell is acquainted with Race & Co., and cognizant of your dealings with them. Now, give him to understand that Mitchell is aware of your presence in Portville, and the whole ground is covered."

Under this arrangement the council was broken up, and twenty minutes after leaving the theater Patterson was again seated beside Sloane, gathering from him the thread of the play, and making himself as agreeable as if no thought of crime and criminals had ever entered his head.

CHAPTER XVII.

Brought to Bay.—The Arrest.

" JIM, here's an old note," said Sloane to Patterson on Monday morning; " I wish you would sell it for me when you sell your bonds."

They were seated in their room, quietly smoking their cigars after a late breakfast, and exchanging an idle word now and then as unconcernedly as though not a scheme or a care was present to

10*

their minds. Patterson was waiting, with secret impatience, for Sloane to urge him to go to the Lank with his bonds, as it was now past eleven o'clock.

As Sloane spoke, he handed Patterson a ragged and much-soiled compound-interest note, mended in two or three places with strips of thin brown paper, pasted over the back, and smelling of must and mildew.

"This looks as though it had seen rough service," said Patterson, examining the note curiously.

"I have had it for a long time; ever since the war," replied Sloane. "I received it when in the army, and carried it in my pistol-pocket for months."

"It has been wet, too," persisted Patterson.

"I should say it had, and my skin beneath it, too!" was the cool reply. "Sell it for what you can get."

"Why, it's past due, and worth all it calls for."

"I know it is, but there will probably be some small discount for the trouble of collecting."

"All right," said Patterson, pocketing the note. "I may as well be off and finish my business with Race at once. Will you come along?"

"If you like, certainly."

Arm in arm they made their way to the bankers', where Mr. Farmer received them with some manifestations of surprise at their early return to Portville. After the exchange of a few words, he led the way to the rear office, where Mr. Race was busy with a mass of books and papers which were scattered recklessly about his desk.

"Ah, Barnes," he exclaimed, without rising from his seat, "you here? How do you do, Mr. Sloane? Glad to see you. Excuse me, gentlemen, for a moment, please. Be seated. There's the Old Harry to pay in Wall street!"

"Why, what's up?" broke in Patterson, eagerly. "I'm interested, you know."

"What's up?" echoed Mr. Race. "Nothing's up. Everything's down. Have you got that Erie yet?"

"Yes, I have," said Patterson, excitedly, "and more, too. What's the price? I saw by the papers it was up two per cent. Saturday."

"Fifty-one," said Mr. Race in reply to Patterson's question. "It fell five per cent. this morning within a half hour!"

"That's terrible!" exclaimed Patterson. "Give me a blank, please. I must telegraph my brokers. They'll be selling me out. Why, this is infernal luck!"

"Here you are, Barnes!" called Mr. Farmer, from the front office. "Step this way."

Patterson hastily rose, and as he passed into the main office, hurriedly said to Sloane:

"Harry, I'm awfully sorry! but I'm afraid you'll have to get along without that money!"

"Humph!" muttered Sloane, with a show of great disappointment.

Mr. Race and Sloane were now alone in the private office, the former still engrossed in the papers before him.

"I shall be back soon, Harry," called out Patterson. "Wait for me, please. I'm only going to the telegraph office."

"Have you a moment to spare, Mr. Race?" inquired Sloane, in a subdued voice, as soon as Patterson had passed into the street.

"Always," replied the banker blandly, as he drew a chair close to his own for his visitor's use. "What can I do for you?"

The hardware merchant's reply was low and distinct. Beyond the partition the sound of his voice could hardly be caught, but within the room it was plainly audible.

"I have some compound-interest notes," replied Sloane, "that I have held for a long time. They have ceased to carry interest, and I want to sell part of them and put the rest in five-twenty bonds. I do not care to have my friend, Barnes, know anything about this, for the reason that he is speculating in stocks, and if he should run short, he would expect me to help him. Ordinarily, I should be very glad to do so, but just now I really need what money I can spare, in my business."

"I think you are quite right in not lending money to a speculator," said Mr. Race, encouragingly. "I make it a rule never to do so myself, unless amply secured. I shall be glad to buy the notes you speak of, or convert them into bonds as you may desire. What amount of them have you ?"

"I have two thousand dollars, which I will bring here in the course of the afternoon. We won't go into particulars now," he said, cautiously and nervously. "I have been trying to borrow some money of Barnes, just to throw him off, you see. He may return here at any moment, and he would think it very unkind of me, if he should discover that I am in funds."

"Let us drop the matter for the present, then," said Mr. Race. "I think he is out there talking with Mr. Farmer, now. State at what time you will call, and I will make it a point to be here."

"Will two o'clock suit you, Mr. Race ?"

"Certainly. Say two o'clock, sharp."

Sloane then drew aside his chair, and assuming

an air and tone of indifference, called out : "Come, Jim ; aren't you ready ?"

"Just ready," returned Patterson, appearing at the door. "Here's the change for that note. They took it at full value, as I supposed they would."

As he spoke, Patterson handed Sloane a small roll of bills, which the latter pocketed with evident satisfaction ; and they then left the office together.

A moment later, one of the great safe-doors, which had been turned back against the wall, swung around slowly, and revealed the portly presence of Superintendent Warner. A broad smile lighted up his naturally genial face as he stepped from his hiding-place, and said to Mr. Race, with warmth :

"Many thanks for your kind and efficient aid. At last we are masters of the situation."

" I am glad if I have been of any service," replied the banker. "When you see Mr. Pinkerton, please give him my compliments, and tell him what an obedient and apt pupil I have been."

"I shall certainly do so," rejoined Mr. Warner, entering into the spirit of the suggestion ; "and I shall take the liberty of recommending you for permanent engagement on our force !"

After the exchange of a few pleasantries of this

kind, Mr. Warner took his leave with the understanding that Race & Co. would, in the afternoon, purchase whatever Sloane might offer them. Using every precaution against the accidental return of Sloane, he then made his way back to the Globe Hotel, where he found detective Wright awaiting him.

Wright reported that Sloane and Patterson intended taking the eight o'clock train in the morning and would return by way of Troydon, as they had come ; Patterson having found it impossible to induce Sloane to return by the way of Ryan.

Mr. Warner immediately telegraphed me the state of affairs, asking what should be done. To this I replied that I would be at Elliott on arrival of the designated train from Portville, and would meet him there. I then telegraphed Mr. Somers to start immediately for Ryan and carry out the programme already conveyed him by one of my detectives.

In the afternoon Sloane sold Messrs. Race & Co. two thousand dollars' worth of compound-interest notes, many of them mildewed and worn like the one handed Patterson, and the entire number bearing evidence of having been for a long time secreted in some damp place or receptacle.

At ten o'clock of the evening of the same day, I left Chicago for Elliott. The time had come when a little wholesome force could be used to advantage ; and as some exceptional responsibility might attach to this, I proposed to conduct the affair in person.

As the express train from Portville rolled into the depot at Elliott, the next day at noon, Mr. Warner and myself stood on the platform, vigilant and ready for action. Mr. Warner, who had come on by the preceding train, had brought me the two thousand dollars in compound interest notes, with the gratifying intelligence that, at last accounts, Sloane had expended none of the money paid him for the same, but carried all of it upon his person. Everything was therefore ripe for my purpose.

Already a goodly number of the incoming passengers had descended to the platform when detective Wright hastened from the rear car and informed us that our parties were there, making very little haste to leave the train, and would probably be the last to appear. This proved to be the case. The bulk of the passengers had left the depot and were far on their different ways, when Patterson and Sloane appeared on the platform, and, with arms interlocked, proceeded to follow the retreating crowd.

"I want you—Come this way!"

It was but the work of an instant to rush in between them, thrust Patterson violently aside, seize Sloane rudely by the wrist and say to him, in a voice of suppressed passion :

"I want you. Come this way !"

In the same breath I shouted to Wright :

"Officer ! bring that man along ; no parleying, now !"

"What does this mean ? this is an outrage !" began Patterson.

We could hear no more, for Wright grasped his prisoner by the collar, taking in his grip shirt, collar and all, and fairly drove him into the baggage-car, while Patterson was seemingly rendered speechless from choking.

As for Sloane, no such angry demonstrations were necessary. He turned deathly pale the instant he recognized me, and began trembling violently from head to foot. So completely did his courage desert him that I had rather to support, than force, him into the same car with Patterson.

It was not to be expected that these arrests could be made without attracting attention. Of necessity, some hubbub and excitement communicated itself to the passengers and employees about the depot, but the whole business was done so quickly that perhaps not more than a half dozen persons witnessed the affair. However many they were, these spread the news with astonishing rapidity, and possibly an annoying disturbance would have ensued, had not Superintendent Warner been on hand to satisfy the curious and quiet agitation by speaking of the fracas as being "merely the arrest of a couple of pickpockets."

I had told the conductor of the outward-bound train, who, in common with nearly all the conductors of the Great Inland road, knew me well, that I had two arrests to make, and, to avoid trouble, would take my prisoners in the baggage-car ; a proposition to which he offered no objection.

"I know what this is for!" faltered Sloane, as he threw himself on a trunk and buried his face in his hands, a picture of abject despondency.

"What do you suppose it is for?" I inquired, ironically, drawing a pair of handcuffs from my pocket and preparing to fasten them upon his wrists. "Let's hear what it is for?"

"The bank robbery," he gasped.

The twenty minutes' stoppage had expired, the bell rang, and we were on our way, not to Troydon, but to Ryan.

"Don't put those things on me, please!" stammered Sloane, in a supplicating way. "I give you my word I will make no effort to escape. I have no reason to do so," he added, gathering courage as he spoke, "for I am not guilty."

"Don't try to play that game on me, young man," I said, sternly, and making the handcuffs secure. "I know all about whether you are guilty or not. If you begin by lying, I promise I will show you no mercy."

"Won't you trust me?" he pleaded. "I will tell you the whole truth whenever you wish to know it. I will go with you peaceably anywhere, but I cannot bear to be manacled in this way."

"I will try you this once," I said, removing the irons; "but remember the first attempt you make to get away will be the last, as sure as my name is Allan Pinkerton!"

I then searched my prisoner thoroughly, emptying his pockets of their entire contents, and satisfying myself that neither in the lining of his clothing nor beneath his undergarments was anything concealed. The fruits of this search were a bunch of keys, some Masonic emblems, a watch and chain, two pocket-books, and lastly, three thousand dollars in compound-interest notes, and twenty-three hundred and eighty dollars in greenback currency.

"Ah!" I exclaimed, as this booty fell into my possession; "no doubt you will be able to account for this trifling amount of pocket-money."

Sloane shook his head in a dull, dejected way, and for a moment made no reply. He was completely unmanned, and I felt pretty certain that I should have but little further trouble with him. Presently, after a visible effort to regain his self-possession, he answered:

"I hope to do so, sir. I came by it honestly."

From the time of entering the car, Patterson had not ceased to mutter his resentment and indignation against what he called " a high-handed outrage." A reckoning day would soon come, he said, and he would be revenged. He would have the law on me. There was nothing whatever against him, and he would show me how much this shameful kidnapping would cost me.

When I thought enough of this sort of talk had been indulged in to give full effect to my powers of intimidation, I turned upon him sharply, and said, with as much ugliness of purpose as I could display : "You sir, take my advice now, and hold your tongue ! You will have all the law you want before I get through with *you.* In the meantime, if you don't behave yourself and keep quiet of your own accord, why, it will be a very simple matter to make you."

A clenched fist and threatening gesture gave point and emphasis to this menace, which seemed to have a good effect ; for, by way of reply, Patterson merely shrugged his shoulders, and gave silent expression to a contemptuous sneer.

"Search that man !" I said sharply to operative Wright ; "more than likely he is in with his friend. He don't look any too honest, that's sure !"

The order was immediately executed, and Wright brought forth, among other things, a package neatly done up and addressed to a well-known banking-house in New York, marked: "Value, $2,000. Per American Express."

"You two gentlemen seem to be tolerably well provided with funds for residents of a small country town !" I observed, as I placed this trophy aside.

"That is my own money," exclaimed Patterson excitedly. "I was to have sent it on by express to New York, as you can see by the address."

"Yes, I know," I said, "and why didn't you send it ?"

"Because my brokers did not require it. I intended sending it to make up a loss on Erie stock. The market rose in the afternoon, and it wasn't necessary."

"You tell a plausible story. Still, I'll keep this for the present, and hold you on suspicion. You are in bad company, and handle altogether too much money for a country insurance agent."

The county sheriff and a constable were at the depot on the arrival of our train at Ryan. I turned my prisoners over to their care, giving strict injunctions in Sloane's hearing that on no account were they to be allowed to communicate with one another.

Sloane now had two or three hours for private meditation in his cell, during which time, Mr. Somers, Mr. Warner, Patterson and myself, discussed the good fare of the Mansion House, and the now pleasant condition of our operation. Mr. Somers was exultant over the turn affairs had taken. He protested that he could not say too much in praise of the Agency, and its schemes, as an offset to past grumblings.

Late in the afternoon, in a private room which the jailer had placed at my service, Sloane was brought before me.

I will not weary the reader with a full account of what transpired at this interview. It lasted over two hours, during the greater part of which time Sloane doggedly asserted his innocence of the robbery itself, and attempted to deceive me with the foolish invention that he had *found* a package of five thousand dollars of compound-interest notes on the Sunday morning following the burglary, in his store, near the Willow street door, where he presumed the robbers had dropped it in their flight. I made use of every argument and instrumentality I could think of to drive him from this story, and impel him to a full confession; but for a long time all was in vain. It was necessary to screen my detective at all hazards. I was, therefore, driven to the use of information, only, that I might have reached through other channels. Still, with these resources alone, I was able to astound Sloane by reference to matters pointing to his guilt. He would show his affright and surprise by involuntary starts and exclamations, but he would not budge from his story. I gave him to understand that Mr. Marston had engaged me to track Barnes, and that I had abandoned the case after bringing it to the point of success, because Mr. Marston insisted upon compromising; a proceeding to which I was unalterably opposed.

This explanation was offered incidentally, as a cover to Patterson, but chiefly to show that I had been for a long time on their joint trail, and to impress upon Sloane the conviction that full restitution was the only basis on which he could treat with me.

It had been constantly reported to me that Sloane was a man of good domestic habits, devoted to his wife, and seemingly appreciative of

home comforts. So, after all other attempts had
proven futile, I strove to reach him through the
medium of his affections. I pictured to him as
best I might, and at great length, the distress that
this affair would cause his friends and relatives,
and most of all, his wife ; and lastly, I spoke of
the danger of his exposure in her then delicate
condition, for, as I understood, he expected to be
shortly a father.

No sooner had I made this reference, than
Sloane, who up to that time had maintained his
old, impassable demeanor, burst into a flood of
tears and cried out :

"Stop, stop! I beg of you ;—I shall go mad.
My poor wife! My dear, innocent, trusting wife !
Oh, heavens! this will kill her !"

Completely overcome, after giving vent to this
wail, he buried his face in his handkerchief and
rocked himself from side to side in an agony of
remorse.

I confess that this spasmodic outburst quite
astonished me. I was far from believing him to
be a man of so deep feeling.

When he had recovered from the violence of
this outbreak, I took up my talk where it had
been broken off, hoping to find the criminal in a
more pliable mood. It seemed, however, that this
man was to disappoint me continually. His tears

and emotional excitement proved to be the beginning and the end of his weakness.

"I pray you desist, Mr. Pinkerton," he said,
with considerable firmness and dignity, "I have
nothing to tell you beyond what you already
know. It is useless to question me further!"

Remembering the fear which Sloane had exhibited at the time of his arrest, and hoping that
he would prove a moral, as well as a physical, coward, I resolved to play my last card.

"It is as you say," I replied, "utterly useless
to question you further, but not for the reason
you imagine." Then, summoning all the stern-
ness of demeanor I could command, I drew closer
to him, and proceeded:

"Henry Sloane, you sit before me this moment
a self-convicted burglar! You have admitted the
taking of five thousand dollars that you knew be-
longed to the bank. That, in itself, constitutes
the crime of robbery, and, for this alone, you are
liable to every penalty of the law, just the same
as if you had broken into the bank vault yourself. Out with the whole truth now, or, by all
that's good, I'll make you regret this day to the
end of your life!"

"You—you have no proof that—that I admitted that," he dared to stammer forth.

"Young man," I rejoined, "I have proof
11

enough to send you to the penetentiary for the rest of your natural life, and there you will go, with your accomplice, if you do not confess everything before leaving this room ! Mr. Somers !"

Never was a man more startled and appalled than was Sloane when he heard this call, and instantly saw Mr. Somers at his elbow. With a great bound he sprang from his chair, and then as quickly sank back again, from the very inability of his muscles to support him.

" I confess," he cried, "it was I who did it, and I alone ! I have the money hidden away ! I will show you where it is !—tell you the whole truth. Oh, my God ! gentlemen, for others' sake than my own be merciful !"

The battle was won !

Without loss of time Sloane told the true story of the robbery. His recital was very long, and covered much with which the reader is already familiar.

Upon the breaking up of our interview, Sloane was placed in a cell with Patterson. No sooner had the jailer left them, than the latter turned upon his unfortunate companion and denounced him with every expression of contempt, as a traitor to friendship, a cheat, and a liar.

"What sort of an animal are you, anyway ?" cried Patterson. "Here for six months I have been trusting you as I would not my own brother, showing you my hand as open as the day, putting it in your power to ruin me at any moment, proving myself to you in every possible way, and yet, with your pockets lined with money, you make a show of being poor and want to borrow a thousand dollars? Is that friendship! Is that confidence?"

"Jim, Jim, you are too hard on me!" faltered Sloane.

"Am I?" retorted Patterson, with a sneer. "What, then, did you want a thousand dollars for? Were you going to beat me out of it, knowing I wouldn't dare sue you? By Jove! Harry Sloane, deep as you are, you have made a terrible mistake to have tried that game on me!"

"Jim, will you listen to me for a moment," said Sloane, pleadingly. "You are altogether wrong about my intentions. I trusted you fully, and would willingly have returned your confidences, but Greene kept cautioning me against it! He made up the scheme of borrowing money from you, just to keep you blinded—not because he was afraid you would willingly betray me, but because, as he said, if he were me he would not trust his own shadow with the secret."

"This is all Greek to me!" interrupted Patterson. "What secret do you mean? What was that money found on you. What under heaven *were* you arrested for ?"

In reply to these questions, Sloane gave my detective substantially the same account of the robbery he had given Mr. Somers and myself, thus confirming the truth of the story in a manner that was irresistible.

"Had you been decently honest with me," said Patterson severely, after a pause, "you never would have got into this scrape. I could have helped you through, sure. This isn't the first time I have been 'in limbo,' as you know. We might have put our heads together long ago, and fixed up a story to account for having so much money, that neither Somers, Pinkerton, nor the devil himself, could shake out of us. But it's all up now. Now the question is, how to make the best of matters as they are ?"

"Yes, yes ; what would you do ?" inquired Sloane, eagerly.

The poor, discomfited man had accepted Patterson's reproaches meekly and without attempting to defend himself in any way. He evidently felt that he had wronged his friend, and merited whatever treatment might come of it. So completely was he humbled that Patterson could not but pity him and gave the following good advice in his kindest tones, which served the purposes of the Agency fully as well as though prompted only by the most disinterested friendship.

"You have just two courses from which to choose ;—one, to deny your guilt, the other, to confess it. In either case, you should pursue the chosen one unflinchingly to the end. You have chosen confession. I think that that was a big mistake. But no matter. It's too late to talk about that. Now, if you are wise, be honest throughout. Your only hope is in the clemency of the bank people. Win this from them by square-dealing. They will not give something for nothing. No one will ;—not even mercy. Relieve them of all trouble ; put them in possession of the rest of the money ; plead guilty on your trial. Save them every expense you possibly can ; and whether you play repentance or not, they will treat you leniently. Now that's my advice. I can't say that I think you deserve it, but I was truthful when I told you a long time ago that it went against the grain for me to turn my back on a friend when he's down !"

"Thanks, Jim, thanks," replied Sloane. "I have treated you badly, I know ; but I am the one who has really to suffer for it. Give me your hand, will you? and believe me when I say that I have not maliciously deceived you at any time."

" There it is," responded Patterson, giving his disconsolate companion a firm pressure of the hand, " and this must be a pledge that whatever may come, you will say nothing of what you know about me."

Such was the parting interview between my detective and his guilty victim. That night they were both taken on to Chicago, and from thence Sloane was hurried over the Great Northern railroad towards Somerset.

CHAPTER XVIII.

Sloane's Confession.—Behind the Bars.—The End.

FROM Sloane's confession I gathered some points concerning the robbery of the Somerset bank, which will be of interest to the reader who has closely followed the circumstances of this remarkably singular operation.

It seems that on the Saturday night before the robbery, Sloane had become engaged to Miss Murdock, to whom he was married shortly afterwards. When he left her house and retired to his room he was naturally in a very happy frame of mind, and remained so as long as he only thought of the pleasures of married life and of none of its perplexities or burdens. But finally he began to consider just how the financial part of it all was going to be arranged, and it had quite a different look to it.

He recollected then that his business was not very prosperous, and that only a few days previous he had learned of the suspension of a large customer who owed him a considerable sum. Soon his thoughts from being of a bright and happy nature, as is often the case, passed to the other extreme, and he became gloomy and despondent. The result was, a restless night with fitful dreams, in which a pitiable condition of trouble and poverty seemed constantly uppermost.

Rising and dressing himself hurriedly in the morning, he quickly left his room for a stroll, hoping to rid himself of these haunting fancies of the night; but as he passed the store, the thought shot into his mind that there, not thirty feet away, was money enough, many times over, to keep his wife and himself in comfort for the rest of their lives. He knew that an unusually large amount of money was in the safe, and also knew the combination of the lock. In five minutes, he thought, he could possess a fortune, if he but dared to take it. The startling, almost overpowering temptation to do so came and went in an instant, and he hurried on, scared and ashamed of even the momentary consideration of so base a project.

It was a bitter cold morning, but the air was bracing and invigorating, and he hoped to shortly dispossess himself of all these wild fancies ; but he had gone but a little way when the thought of the pile of money in the bank, and the ease with which it could be taken, came back with double force, and with it the dream of poverty and trouble. He tried to fight it all from him but was unsuccessful, and then, after a time, he set himself deliberately about following these desperate thoughts wherever they might lead him ; and it occurred to him that he could do this more calmly and deliberately in the store than out upon the street.

Turning on his heel, he took his way back to the store, half-unconsciously, and altogether without definite purpose other than to think the matter over fully.

When he entered the store he was certain of having no intention to commit the robbery. But as soon as he saw the safe standing there before him, with its vast sum of money so easily accessible, then some inward prompting, call it the devil if you will, seemed to whisper to him :

"Now is the time. Take it quickly. No one will ever suspect *you !*"

Then, for an instant, there flashed upon him thoughts of the comforts and luxuries he could lavish upon his wife ; the life of ease and happiness they might lead—if he only dared to take that money !

The rest was only a blank to him, and he could not recollect what thoughts shot back and forth like swift shuttles through his brain ; but all were finally swept away by the consciousness of his power, and the opportunity of gaining instant wealth.

As I have stated, the combination was known to him. He had seen the cashier, Mr. Norton, repeatedly open the safe, and had had impressed on his mind, by mere force of constant observation, the figures on the disk and the requisite order and number of revolutions, but, as he stated—and I believe he told the truth—without any effort of will, and without any conscious purpose.

When the gleam of riches so easily to be acquired burst upon him, he stepped towards the safe, slowly and deliberately opened the lock, turned the bolts, and, in an instant, a fortune was exposed to view. Before him were several packages of national bank notes and legal tenders, and

11*

on the floor of the safe were two tin boxes which he knew contained United States seven-thirties and compound-interest notes. Without a moment's hesitation he placed them all on the cashier's desk.

Then, and not till then, did he realize that he was committing a robbery, that there was danger of detection, and necessity for dispatch. The plate at the back of the lock caught his eye. He unfastened it, removing the screws with his penknife, and then tried to change the combination. Fearful of losing too much time, he forsook this purpose almost immediately, as he had some vague notion that throwing the combination off would give the impression that the safe had been broken into by burglars.

He then closed the safe, secreted the currency about his clothing, wrapped up the tin boxes in a couple of newspapers, went to the stable, leaving the store-door open behind him, and placed his parcels in a light wagon he intended using in driving out to his sister's, some little distance in the country.

By this time it was eight o'clock, and Sloane hastened home to breakfast.

The family were at table when he entered. He remarked casually that his sister had written him to visit her, which was true, and that he was going that morning, having already hitched up the horse.

With this excuse he hurried from the table, and drove to his brother-in-law's house, arriving there about noon. In the evening Sloane was left alone with his sister, the rest of her family, the husband and two children, having gone to church. Making the excuse that he wished to look after his horse, he went to the stable, took the tin boxes from the wagon, broke one of them open, and placed in it all the bank money he had about him, which so filled the box that the lid would not close. He then got a spade, went to a point in the woods about a hundred yards from the stable, and there buried the treasure with all possible haste. Before the family returned from church, he had returned to the house, nor was he gone long enough to excite his sister's curiosity.

The next day he drove into Somerset about noon. Before he reached home he was stopped many times, and told of the robbery, and he easily gathered that no suspicion attached to his movements, nor to himself.

Sloane stated that he had only been to the place where he deposited the money once since that time. He then discovered that the notes in

the open box had become all mildewed and
weatherworn. He took out enough of the worst
of them to enable him to close the box, and these
he afterward secreted in his stable in Somerset.
He also opened the other box, and took three
thousand dollars in compound-interest notes from
the same, two thousand of which he sold in Chicago. The other one thousand he exchanged and
expended in Troydon when on visits there with
Patterson.

When he started out on this last trip to Portville, he took with him a five thousand dollar
package of compound-interest notes from the
stable, as all the greenbacks and national bank
currency were in so rotten a condition that he
dared not attempt to pass it. Two thousand of
this five thousand he sold to Messrs. Race & Co.,
of Portville. The proceeds of this sale, together
with the remaining three thousand dollars of compound-interest notes, were taken from him at the
time of his arrest.

Such is the story of the robbery, summarized
from a much longer narrative written out by
Sloane.

To me its most striking feature was that it
made no mention of Greene, nor of any accomplice. I had pressed this point upon Sloane in

our interview at Ryan as strongly as I knew how, but to no purpose. He denied most positively that any one had been concerned with him, and was particularly earnest in exculpating Greene from even a guilty knowledge of his crime. He admitted that Greene might have suspected the truth with regard to it, for the subject had never been discussed between them without reserve, as it would have been had both been innocent; but he stated, on the other hand, that Greene had not profited, nor attempted to profit, one penny by his voluntary concealment of whatever suspicion he might have.

Nothing different from this could be wrung from Sloane, and I was compelled to accept his statement for what it was worth. Through his admissions to Patterson I know that he was screening Greene more than the facts would warrant. I knew that the secret of the crime was a matter very well understood between them, and that Greene had directly aided and abetted him, at least by caution and advice, in the disposition of the plunder; but this was all I did know.

It was very strange that Greene should have given so many indications of criminality and still be innocent; but it must be remembered that the knowledge of another's crime, if wickedly kept

secret, often acts upon the human mind similar to
the consciousness of guilt. It may be assumed,
from Greene's quick perceptive powers, and natural keenness, that he had at an early date become aware of the truth concerning the robbery,
and that then Sloane's actions and general bearing, as well as his admissions, soon gave his surmises the force of absolute knowledge ; or, it may
have been possible that, notwithstanding Sloane's
assertions to the contrary, he had directly revealed
his guilt to his partner. One or the other theory
seemed necessary to account for the conduct on
Greene's part which had for so long a time kept
me on the wrong trail. Accepting then the second alternative I dismissed the matter from my
mind as a mere speculative study, void of practical significance. It was a fact that Greene had
not profited by the crime, nor had I any proof
that he was an accessory.

Sloane kept his promise of restitution fully
and in good faith. My son Robert and myself
took him from Chicago to the residence of his
brother-in-law, there recovered the bank's treasure, which we found buried as stated, and then
proceeded to Somerset, where I gave up both prisoner and plunder to the authorities.

Sloane also made over to Mr. Somers all his

interest in the hardware business, and gave up every article of value in his possession, including the jewelry and other expensive articles purchased for his wife with the bank's money; but these were surrendered very reluctantly, and not until his wife had herself earnestly urged that it should be done. Thus the apparent loss to the bank was largely reduced, and when the accounts were finally made up, Mr. Somers informed me that the deficit was but trifling, inclusive of the expenses of the operation.

From the time of his confession to the end Sloane seemed far worse broken down by the ruin of his domestic happiness than by the pangs of conscience. On the journey to Somerset he would repeatedly break forth with expressions of despairing pity for his wife; and constantly sought to devise means to keep her from a knowledge of the terrible shame and degradation that had fallen upon him. He begged me to allow Patterson to break the news to her, lest the shock should prove too great for her to bear, and endanger her life. In refusal of this request I felt compelled to inform him that his friend was in captivity at Chicago, awaiting a requisition from the Governor of New York; that I had telegraphed the fact of his arrest to that city and had received instructicns to hold him until the necessary papers could be forwarded. Sloane thereupon expressed the deepest regret that his guilt should have been the means of getting a tried and trusted friend into trouble, but consoled himself with the remark that even were Patterson guilty he would never be convicted, as he was far too shrewd to leave his tracks uncovered.

With the surrender of a criminal to justice, and the transfer to rightful owners of whatever property may have been recovered, my direct connection with an operation ceases. An interest, however, is always excited that continues to the final disposition of each case ; and, outside of this, it is important in a business point of view that I should know as much as possible of the history of criminals. Being so advised, my clients rarely report the concluding incidents connected with matters once under our investigation ; and, in this way, the records of my Agencies compass a more or less complete account, up to prison gates, of the life of every individual offender who may have been brought to justice through its instrumentality.

So it came that in the latter part of April I learned through Mr. Somers that Sloane had pleaded guilty to the charge of larceny, and had been sentenced to three years' imprisonment in the Michigan Penitentiary, at Jackson.

In consideration of his straightforward conduct from the time of his confession, the bank officials had sanctioned the most lenient treatment of the criminal they could bring themselves to regard as justifiable. Hence the charge of larceny instead of burglary, and hence so light a sentence ; which, after all, may seem sufficient punishment when it is remembered that not only this had to be endured, but that his business was utterly ruined, his property completely absorbed, and his domestic happiness, though his brave little wife clung to him through it all, shattered beyond repair ; while everything that a man of feeling loves, prizes or prides himself upon in an honorable career, was forever at an end.